Praise for Shiloh Walker's
Beautiful Scars

"This wonderfully evocative story manages to meld an emotional and very sensitive subject with a delightfully sensual exploration between lovers. [...] Another delicious story from a talented storyteller."

~ *Night Owl Reviews*

"I was blown-away by *Beautiful Scars*. Ms. Walker had me at 'hello' as the old saying goes. [...] She wrote a love story that takes your breath away and has tears in your eyes throughout the story for both of the main characters."

~ *Guilty Pleasures Book Reviews*

"The book had the perfect amount of sexual chemistry and compatibility, it was really sizzling off the pages! [...] This is a hot but also sweet story that I think you will definitely love!"

~ *Under the Covers Book Blog*

Look for these titles by
Shiloh Walker

Now Available:

Talking with the Dead
Always Yours
For the Love of Jazz
Beautiful Girl
Vicious Vixen
Playing for Keeps
My Lady
The Redeeming
No Longer Mine
A Forever Kind of Love
The Unwanted

The Hunters
The Huntress
Hunter's Pride
Malachi
Hunter's Edge

Grimm's Circle
Candy Houses
No Prince Charming
I Thought It Was You
Crazed Hearts
Tarnished Knight
Locked in Silence
Grimm Tidings
Blind Destiny

Print Collections
Legends: Hunters and Heroes
Taking Chances
The First Book of Grimm
The Second Book of Grimm
Lost in Love

Beautiful Scars

Shiloh Walker

Samhain Publishing, Ltd.
11821 Mason Montgomery Road, 4B
Cincinnati, OH 45249
www.samhainpublishing.com

Beautiful Scars
Copyright © 2014 by Shiloh Walker
Print ISBN: 978-1-61921-633-4
Digital ISBN: 978-1-61921-456-9

Editing by Tera Kleinfelter
Cover by Lyn Taylor

First Samhain Publishing, Ltd. electronic publication: January 2013
First Samhain Publishing, Ltd. print publication: January 2014

Dedication

For my kids and husband, always. I love you.

Chapter One

"You're supposed to go to a party tonight."

Marc Archer stopped in the middle of the song, the melody that had been dancing in the back of his mind crashing to an abrupt halt. "A party," he muttered. Then he remembered. "Oh. Yeah. Caleb's thing. Selene was going with me."

"Hmmm. Yes. She was, that was the plan."

Lifting his head, he stared at the angelic face of the woman who put up with his cranky, forgetful ass and basically made his world continue to function. Her name was Ilona Muñoz and if she wasn't married to one of his best friends, he just might have married her himself. Not that she'd have him or anything, but he'd try. Just because she made life so much easier for him. When she wasn't driving him crazy.

Because he thought better when he played, and because he knew she had a weakness for the song, he fell into a classical piece by Philip Glass, smiling a little as her brows dropped low over her eyes. "You play dirty, Marc," she muttered.

"I didn't know we were playing a game." He continued to play and waited.

"Yeah, yeah. Well, your pleather-wearing Barbie doll can't do the party. She actually left a message. It was in the mailbox when I got here." Her eyes fell away and she suddenly took a serious interest in her nails. "I...uh...well. Here."

She dropped a piece of paper on top of the Steinway and turned around, moving out of the studio so quick, she might as well have been running. She reached the door and looked back at him. "I'm sorry. I...well. I know you two had a thing for a while."

Marc reached for the note.

A thing.

Hell.

What did he and Selene have exactly?

He met her at Blue's, a local club that catered to those with...unusual tastes; it was crazy expensive and beyond private. Getting a membership was harder than hell. The members were expected to respect the privacy of other members, the one reason he felt somewhat safe indulging there.

Selene understood the kind of games he played; she got the rules, because they were her rules too. She wasn't out to jerk him around, because he could do the same thing to her. It was safe that way. He'd played the game only with people who had a need to be just as careful as he was.

It was a lesson he'd learned the hard way.

He didn't love Selene, but he liked her. Respected her. Enjoyed her.

Still, it was a bit of a punch to look at the note and read:

Marc,

We've had fun. But I've met somebody and I think it could be real. I know you needed me for something tonight, but I can't keep this up when I've got a chance for something better.

S

Folding the note back up, he dropped it on the bench next to him. It wasn't even noon. He'd worry about the damn party later.

Resting his hands back on the keys, he fell back into the music. It was better there, anyway.

"I need a date."

Leaning back in her chair, Shera MacNeil sighed and picked up her nail file. As she stroked it along her index finger, she studied the man in front of her desk. It wasn't terribly unusual for people to just show up in the office of *Escortè*, the companion service she'd taken over from her mother.

She provided a service. Companionship. Phone calls, dates, that sort of thing. Nothing else, although there were more than a few who thought otherwise. Her ladies, and the few men she kept on call, kept their clothes on. Period. Or they were terminated. Period.

Her employees knew that. The clients knew that. It was a good arrangement and a service that was highly in demand.

Most people called, though. Or used the Internet.

It was just more convenient. And easier for her when they didn't pass her rather strict vetting.

The man in front of her had passed the vetting. He was also a repeat customer, despite his surly attitude and penchant for showing up late. The women she paired him with had to be damn good at conversation, because he *sucked* at it and the only time he ever needed her services was when he was going to some sort of party where he had to socialize. He used the companion to do all the talking for him, so he could do what he did best...stand there and brood. Until he got talked into playing or singing.

He was tall, pushing six foot three, and he was attractive enough, she figured. More than a few of her employees would love to be his companion for the night—and not just the women. But she had this little thing with people just barging in like this.

Especially *this* guy. He was about impossible to pair up with any of her ladies, despite being a great-looking guy, despite being a good tipper.

Lately, he hadn't needed her company much and she'd hoped that would continue. Damn her luck, anyway. Studying his surly expression, she leaned back in her chair and crossed one leg over the other.

Well, surly or not, money was money. She'd spent too many years broke not to appreciate how much easier money could make things.

"When do you need a companion, Marc?"

"Tonight. I've got a big party and the woman I was taking decided to bail."

"Hmm. Is this a temporary thing or a permanent thing?"

He bared his teeth at her.

She smiled back. "I'll take that to mean it's permanent. Damn. Such a shame. It must have something to do with your charming personality."

"Are you going to help me or not? I can't go alone." He shoved a hand through his hair, but the thick, dark locks promptly fell back into his eyes. He needed a haircut. Something he usually put off until he couldn't do it any longer and then he attacked it himself with a pair of scissors he found lying around the house. Which then required professional help to fix the damage before he went back on the road. Always fun.

"Now, Marc...you know I can't go out on a date with you," she chided. "That would be rather disgusting, seeing as how you're my half-brother."

"Ha, ha." He flung himself into a chair and glared at her. "Are you going to help me out or not, Sher? I need a date for this party. If I go alone..." His voice trailed off and he hunched his shoulders a little, his mouth twisting into a scowl.

He didn't need to elaborate.

She knew. Marc had a bad habit of ending up in trouble with females if he wasn't careful. Hell. He ended up in trouble even when he *was* careful. Sometimes she thought he was living under some sort of hellish curse or something, the luck he had going on lately.

He sat up, braced his elbows on his knees and twined his fingers. Staring down at the carpet, he asked in a flat voice, "Are you going to help?"

Before she could answer, the door opened.

Shera sighed, a headache of massive proportions building at the base of her skull as her best friend came to a dead stop. Chaili Bennett saw Marc, her eyes popped wide and she slipped back out. "Hmm. Bad timing. Hey, Marc. I'll just go to the back and get myself some coffee."

As the door closed behind Chaili, Marc got to his feet.

The siblings shared very few features in common. He was big, dark and had the brooding musician bit down to an art. Seeing as how he was wowing people on stage, putting out songs that steadily ranked high on the charts and was pretty much on the road to becoming a rock legend, she guessed the brooding artist thing wasn't altogether bad.

Shera was petite, like their mother had been, and so fair she burned any time she spent more twenty minutes outside without SPF-50 slathered on. At least it seemed that way.

But they both had the same dark hair, the same eyes...Mom's eyes. Pale gold, ringed with a rim of near black, surrounded by dark spiky lashes. He was older than her by two

13

years. She adored him. He'd been the one who'd taught her how to ride a bike, had been the one to walk her home in grade school, waiting for her after he'd gone on to middle school. He'd helped her with algebra and lit, and the fact that she'd bombed chemistry was totally his fault, but that was okay, because why in the hell did she need chemistry, anyway?

She'd been in her sophomore year and he'd been a senior before things got easier at home and their single mother hadn't had to work so many long hours. Still, Shera would never forget how many years it had been them. Just them.

Sighing, she said, "What time?"

Hiding in the kitchen, Chaili leaned against a counter and tried to make herself breathe. It was just Marc, after all. She knew him almost as well as she knew Shera, although half of the known world would scoff if she tried to claim that.

She'd known him when he'd been a struggling musician, playing in bars, at weddings, in the worst hellhole clubs known to man. And she'd loved him then.

She loved the way those slow, reluctant smiles would tug at the corners of his mouth.

She loved the way he expressed himself through music, because he was so hesitant to do it any other way.

She loved the way he adored his sister and their mother.

She loved the way he could be sitting in a room, seemingly oblivious to everything going on while he worked on a song, and then out of the blue, he could just jump in on a conversation and drop a line that could pretty much either turn the discussion on its head or stop it completely.

She loved the way he tried to think things through before

he said a damn thing, a habit he'd started developing in the latter part of high school. He had what Shera and Chaili teasingly called *Open Mouth Insert Foot* disorder...a very blunt of way of stating things that had often landed him in trouble— with his mom, in school, with his friends, with his girlfriends, in his jobs, in life...

Not so much now with his professional life, because he tended to just stay quiet unless he had no other choice, or dole out bits and pieces through carefully worded press releases written by others.

She loved the way he didn't feel like he had to do that so much around her. Not that she ever saw him anymore. Because he rarely came home.

Damn, she missed him. And instead of being able to go in there and talk to him for at least a minute, she was in here hiding, because something was bothering him. She'd seen it.

Glumly, she made her way over to the coffeemaker and poured herself a cup. Hell, if she hadn't seen a mention of it on the news, she wouldn't even know he was in town. He never emailed anymore. Ever since she'd stopped doing his website, it was like...

"Don't think about this," she muttered. It was sometimes *too* depressing to think about.

Not that she was upset he was doing so well. She was happy for him. He'd wanted so badly to make it with his music and he'd done it. He had a face that was regularly splashed across the Internet, and last year he'd been in the running for one of those crazy *World's Sexiest Bachelor* things. His band was one of the most popular ones in the country...hell, in the *world* right now. She was happy for him.

But she missed her friend. And her heart ached for the bits and pieces she used to be able to console herself with.

The door to the kitchen swung open and Shera appeared there. The other woman's gaze locked on the cup of coffee. "Gimme."

Hunching over the cup, Chaili made a face. "Get your own."

"I only made enough for one more cup. I was supposed to be the only one here today."

Staring into Shera's golden eyes, Chaili lifted the cup and took a slow, happy sip. As she lowered it, she smiled at her friend. "You make awesome coffee, woman."

"You're such a bitch. Everybody thinks you're so damn sweet, but I know better." She sighed and reached for the coffee beans. "What are you doing here?"

"Stopped by to talk to you about the updates on your site." Chaili nodded toward her laptop bag sitting by the door. She had a website design company and one of her biggest clients was staring at the coffeemaker like it was capable of creating pure gold out of nothing. "You'd mentioned you wanted some pictures so I was going to take a few and see if I can get a feel for what you wanted."

"Oh." Shera rubbed the back of her neck, a gesture that was oddly familiar—Marc did that all the time when he was stressed or thinking. "Yeah, I think you mentioned that. My brother's gone and fried my brain. Again."

"Hmmm." Chaili settled back against the wall, recalling how Marc had looked earlier. Well, other than gorgeous. He always looked gorgeous. With that blacker-than-black hair, the perpetual five o'clock shadow, the elegant, almost beautiful lines of his face...and those hands... She managed, just barely to swallow her sigh before it escaped.

"Would you quit that already?"

Jerking her head up, she found Shera looking at her. "Quit what?"

"You're thinking about my brother again." Shera made a face. "If you're going to think about him that much, just ask him out, damn it."

Chaili grimaced. She'd tried that. Three times. Failed. Three times. Wasn't going to try for a fourth failure. Forcing herself to smile easily, she shrugged. "Sweetheart, I've tried that and it didn't take. He's not interested. Besides, half the females between fourteen and forty-five probably think about your brother at some point in their lives. Deal with it."

"It's a little bit different when the woman *knows* him." She gave Chaili a pointed stare. "You do. You didn't go and turn him into a sex object."

"Your brother was born a sex object," she said, trying to keep the subject lighter than it really was. No. Marc wasn't a sex object for her. He was her everything. And he had no interest in her at all. That was life. "So, what did the sex object want?"

"I'm going to hit you. Just so you know." Shera sighed and tucked her hair behind one ear, reaching for the bag of coffee beans. Once she had another pot brewing, she walked over to the table, dropped into the seat and promptly thunked her head on the table. "He needs a date."

Chaili's jaw dropped.

She was still staring at her best friend as the woman thunked her head two or three more times.

By the fourth time, the words had penetrated. In sympathy for the headache Shera was going to give herself, she went over to the table, and before Shera could bang her head a fifth time, she caught the woman's shoulders. "Your brother wants to use the service?" she asked.

That just didn't seem to mesh. Settling into the seat next Shera, she studied the brunette.

"Why in the world would he want to use the service?"

Shera closed her eyes and slumped in the seat. "Don't worry about it, Chaili. It's a complicated mess but I'll work it out."

"Too complicated to tell me?" She nudged Shera with her shoulder. "I'm your best friend, right? It's not like I'm going to sell the story to *The Sun* or *People* or *The National Enquirer.*" She stopped, pursed her lips. "Well, I could sell it to *The National Enquirer*. It's not like I don't need the money. I'd have to slum it up a little. You know...alien babies, Elvis was seen at his house, that sorta thing."

Shera tipped her head back, laughing. "Yeah. That might work." Sighing, she said, "Look, Marc's dating thing is...well, like I said—complicated, okay? He just prefers to use the service because it's a little less..." Abruptly, Shera snapped her mouth shut. "Never mind."

But Chaili was already gaping at her. "He *prefers* to use the service...you mean this isn't the first time you've set him up on a date?"

Shera stood. "I'm probably going to be late getting home. Maybe we should do pizza tomorrow instead."

They had a standing date for pizza on Fridays, although if one of them had a date, they moved it. Usually it was Shera who had the date. Chaili thought she might have had a date sometime around the last ice age. No...wait. There had been a few after her spectacular failure of a marriage.

Just a few. But she preferred to block that period of her life out.

Realizing her chance to pry loose some details about Marc was about to walk out the door, Chaili jumped up and jogged over to the door, all but barring Shera's way. "Let me do it."

"Do what?"

Chaili just stared at her friend, crossing her arms over her chest.

Finally, it clicked and Chaili watched as Shera's mouth dropped open. "You're not serious."

Her instinct was to hunch up her shoulders. Instead, she gave a half shrug. "Hey, why not? It's not like I don't know how to talk to him."

"*He* won't be the problem. He's going to a big party thing up on the Mile."

Chaili arched her brows. "I've been to parties up on the Mile before," she drawled. More than she cared to count. Cocking her head, she smiled. "If that's the plan for the night, I'd actually be perfect. I know how to make small talk. I can dress up all nice and pretty and Marc knows me."

That was all Shera's service provided, really. Companionship, conversation. Chaili could chat pretty damn well, if she had to, and she could also dress up pretty. She had a few pieces—a very few, that would work for a party on the Mile.

Shera hesitated.

"Come on. Let me help you with this," she said.

"Not a good idea, sweetie." Shera edged around her, heading back to her office.

"Why not?" She strolled along after Shera, her longer legs keeping up with Shera's fast strides easily. She wanted to do this, damn it. It was just a date. One date. She could have one date with him, right?

"It's just not." Back in her office, Shera dropped into her seat and glanced up at Chaili. "I'm going to be busy for a while. I need to go through my files and figure out who isn't going to drive him totally insane."

"Why? *I* would work."

"No." Shera glared at her. "Damn it, Chaili, I know you've got a thing for him, but it won't work. Trust me, the two of you would have...incompatibilities."

Incompatibilities. Chaili sighed. "Look, I'm not asking you to arrange a marriage. It's just a date. He needs somebody for the party, right?" Forcing herself to smile, she shrugged. "Why not me?"

The two women just stared at each other as seconds ticked away and finally Shera groaned. "Shit. Fine. All right. I'm being stupid, anyway. It's a date and you're right. You're probably the best qualified to go out with him, considering the only other women I'd trust to do it are already booked. The others..." She trailed off, grimacing. "They'd love to do it and then they'd see who he was, try to get his pants off and then despite the confidentiality clause, they'd blab their mouth. I'd have my hands full shutting their traps and..."

"Shera...?"

Shera snapped her mouth shut.

Chaili smiled. She absolutely was *not* going to say that she'd love to get into Marc's pants. She wasn't going to say it. She might think it. She might dream about it. *Often.* But she wasn't going to say it. And even if that miracle ever happened, she'd sure as hell never blab about it.

"So...what all am I supposed to do?"

"You really want to do this."

Settling into the chair across from the desk, Chaili tried not to look too eager. That wouldn't be good. At all. Crossing one leg over the other, she smiled. "Sure. It's not like we can't order pizza tomorrow. And I like Marc."

Love him. I've always loved him...

Shera stared at her, grim-faced, but although she might have seen straight through Chaili's lie, she didn't call her on it. Instead, she bent down, opened a drawer. Ten seconds later, Chaili found herself staring at a contract.

"Sign it."

Chaili arched her brows. "Seriously?"

With a narrow look, Shera leaned forward. "Yes. If you're doing this, you're doing it by the book...including the contract. You'll get the standard fee, because *yes*, the few times he's come through here and needed to use the place, he has paid. It's all on the up-and-up and you know I don't allow any bullshit in my place. That goes for you too. If you're serious about doing this, sign the damn contract."

Chaili rolled her eyes. And as she reached for the pen, she hoped her fingers weren't shaking.

"Now, what do you have to wear?"

Chapter Two

At the piano, head bent, Marc lost himself to the music.

Once upon a time, he'd let himself get lost in other places, hadn't worried about anything but the moment. He'd just...lived.

The last time had been years ago—it had ended with Lily. He didn't let himself think about her often, because that had been a hot fucking mess. They'd worked together—she'd been his manager for years and they'd been friends.

Then he'd been stupid enough to let it become something more. He'd thought it was all just fine too. Six good months. Actually, six wonderful months, then he'd walked in and found her in a rather compromising position—her on her knees with her mouth wrapped around another man's dick, her hands tied behind her back. It wasn't the position he minded—but the fact that she'd been going down on another man, well, that posed a problem. And the guy had also been a friend of his.

Both of them had tried to convince him he'd taken it too personally.

Then Lily had tried to convince him that if he walked...

The music broke around him and he stopped, closed his eyes and let his hands rest on the keys for a minute. This was why he didn't let himself think about that. It wasn't even that she'd fucked around on him. He'd been cheated on before. It sucked and he hated it, but he could have handled that.

It was what she'd tried to do after.

How messed up things had gotten.

That was why he didn't let himself go anymore. It just wasn't safe.

Better off not to lose himself like that anymore. Unless it was the music. He could trust the music.

Clearing his mind, he focused on the song he could *almost* hear in his mind. The melody was clearer now, and it came easily. The words, though, he was still waiting on them.

Inner demon

How you fight...

Another line of it came to him and he stopped playing to jot it down before going back to the keys. Before another sixty seconds passed, his phone beeped. His connection to the world, that stupid thing. Sometimes he hated it. Mostly he needed it. Ilona kept it up to date, all his appointments and everything programmed into the calendar. If he didn't have something to remind him where he was supposed to be and what he needed to be doing, he'd be screwed.

Although he'd rather not remember he had plans for tonight.

Fuck the party.

So what if his manager thought he should go to that damn party? Bryan had taken over Lily's job a few years ago, and Marc had to admit, the guy did a good job. He knew what he was doing, business-wise.

He was okay. Marc liked him. The guys from the band liked him. He generally knew what he was talking about, too, when it was came to the PR shit. A few weeks ago Bryan had called him—there was a benefit going on for autism and Marc should go. Marc would rather not go to any damn party and had tried to just send a donation, but that wasn't what Bryan wanted. So

Marc was going to the damn benefit. The one thing about the party that didn't entirely suck—it was being thrown by another friend, Caleb Wickham. Seeing Caleb wouldn't be bad and at least the guy didn't throw boring parties.

But Marc would much rather stay home.

If he'd known how things were going to turn out—Selene dropping him at the last minute, hell... He would have told Bryan to shove the benefit up his ass.

Even with a date lined up from his sister's service, the night was going to be a pain in the ass. Staying at home sounded so much better. He could work on his music. Maybe even just go over to Shera's.

A faint smile curled his lips as he pushed back from the piano. It was Friday, after all. That meant only one thing—pizza and movies.

Chaili.

He should have at least said hi to her earlier. She'd disappeared before he had a chance, but he'd been irritated, frustrated, pissed off. By the time he'd gotten around to thinking about anything more than the fiasco that was sure to happen tonight, he'd already been five miles away.

He'd been in town for four days and he hadn't even called her to say hi. They never talked anymore and he missed her. Hell, if he had half a brain, he should have just thought about it and called her for tonight. It didn't have to be a date. He just needed a woman with him at the party, otherwise he wouldn't be able to breathe, or move. The last time he'd gone to a party solo, one woman had actually paid a cab driver to follow him to his hotel and she'd tried to bribe the people at the front desk.

Marc had actually been standing a few feet behind her— he'd managed to deactivate his damn keycard and needed another one. Lucky him, because the hundred-dollar bill the girl had pushed toward the guy behind the desk had apparently looked enticing. Although it might have been the D cups she'd been flashing.

Scowling at the memory, he headed into the bedroom to check his reflection one more time. Thanks to his assistant, he didn't have to worry about just wearing T-shirts, jeans, and black or red nonstop. His sister and a few others knew he was color-blind.

Personally, he figured *color deficient* or something would be more accurate. He could see plenty of colors. Reds were awesome. He could see them just fine. Blues worked. He liked blue too. Oranges, though, they blended to red for him. Yellows were a mess, and so was green. Greens all blurred into blue for him.

It didn't matter personally to him and it wasn't a big deal, the way he saw it. Yeah, he'd had some trouble in school with it until he'd picked up on the variation in hue and brightness. Plus, *reading* the color on the crayons and shit had helped.

He hadn't even realized he'd had the problem until later in life, anyway.

The biggest issue it caused for him was accidentally pairing a yellow tie with a green shirt or something. Easiest if he could stick with black and red, and he tended to do that a lot.

The clothes had labels and everything was coordinated. *Goes with jacket #4, #16, #22,* etc., etc. Made it easy on him. But tonight he hadn't been in the mood to root through the damn closet. It wasn't a date for him and he didn't care what his "companion" thought. She was getting paid nearly a grand to put up with his cranky ass and to keep her mouth shut about it.

As for the people at the party...they wouldn't care anyway. The black silk shirt, a pair of black jeans...that worked well enough for him. The black leather Italian shoes were an indulgence he allowed himself on pretty much any occasion that suited. A party was definitely an occasion. A quick look in the mirror showed a familiar sight. Him, his hair too long, stubble—he'd forgotten to shave. Again. He didn't have time to mess with it now. His sister would kick his ass if he was late.

"Shit, knowing her, she'd charge me double," he grumbled.

Not that he couldn't afford it, but after so many years of growing up with barely enough money to scrape by...yeah, he wasn't going to pay *that* kind of money just because she felt like charging him.

And again, he could have avoided it if he'd given Chaili a call. He doubted she'd mind wasting a night at some dumb-ass party. Wasn't like she ever did much other than pizza and movies with Shera, right?

They could have caught up. Had a decent night and he would definitely have had more fun with her than whomever Shera had found.

He frowned, wondering if it was too late to call the companion thing off. So what if he had to pay for it? He could call Chaili and ask if she had plans...

Then he sighed.

It was already after six. He was supposed to be at the office at seven.

Under his breath, he muttered, "Any reason why you couldn't have this idea, oh, say, four hours ago?"

There was no answer. Just the endless, empty silence of his house.

Chaili smacked at Shera's hands as she went to adjust the

halter-styled bodice of the white cocktail dress Chaili had ended up picking from her miniscule selection. The bra she had to wear with it was irritating the *hell* out of her, but if she didn't wear it, it wouldn't fit right.

That, on top of Shera's fussing, was just edging on her last nerve.

"Would you leave me *alone?*" Chaili snapped. Damn it, Shera was fussing over her like a mother hen. You'd think it was her first date or something. *It's not a real date,* she reminded herself. He'd paid for it. And he didn't know *she* was the one going out with him. Taking a deep breath, she went back to staring at her reflection. Oh, hell. She wasn't really doing this, was she?

"Stop being a bitch," Shera said. "And breathe, damn it."

"Stop being an old mother hen!" Nudging her away, Chaili went back to staring at her reflection. The woman in the mirror was somebody she barely recognized. She hadn't seen much of this woman in the past few years. Back when she'd been married, she'd had to do the cocktail party round often. Tim had been big into socializing and she hadn't much cared...at first.

The woman in front of her didn't exactly look the same. And she wasn't. She was leaner. Harder. Stronger.

And scarred.

Not that the scars were easily seen, but still...

She adjusted the dress, smoothing it a little and twisting to make sure it laid the right way. "It looks pretty good, don't you think?"

"Yep. That's a great style on you, sweetie. And you practically glow. I'd kill to tan like that." Shera smiled and rested her cheek on Chaili's arm.

"Sunless tanner works just fine, ya know. Not all of them turn you that carroty orange." She reached up and brushed her fingers through her hair. The choppy, asymmetrical cut fell right back into place, framing her face. She'd let Shera do her makeup and she had to admit, the woman knew her stuff. The bronze and blue eyeshadow wasn't anything Chaili normally would have done on her own but it worked, accentuating her blue eyes, which were admittedly her best feature.

That and her mouth. She had a decent mouth, wide and soft, and right now it was tinted a deep, lush wine color. Again, not anything she would have chosen herself, but Shera knew her stuff. It was a henna-based dye that would supposedly last all night. Not that Chaili expected to do anything to challenge the dye's staying power. Slicking her tongue over her lips, she took a deep breath and sighed. "Here goes nothing, I guess."

She squared her shoulders and met Shera's gaze in the reflection. "He's not going to freak out when he sees me, is he?"

"A little late to worry about that now, isn't it?" Shera flashed her a grin. Then she shrugged. "Relax. You two are friends. It will throw him for a minute, I bet, but he needed a date. I didn't really have anybody available that wouldn't end up in a disaster, so this is it. Relax. We're good."

We're good. Chaili squared her shoulders. They were good.

But the butterflies dancing in her belly weren't exactly comforted. She placed a hand over her abdomen to calm them and turned away from her reflection. No matter how long she stared, she wasn't going to change the woman she saw staring back at her anyway, right?

The office was tucked away not far from his home in Lake Forest. Marc knew most of the people in the area had an idea just what *Escortè* did, and he suspected a few of them also thought there was more to the companionship service that his sister offered. He also knew she had her hands full chasing away the idiots who weren't convinced by the office policy. He'd seen their mother dealing with it before she retired, had watched Shera handling it off and on, had listened to some of her stories, ranging from the funny to the fucked-up.

Personally, he was glad he had an in to the place.

It made his life easier.

He could play the dating game okay, but he got tired of trying to do it. It was easier for him to keep it impersonal, professional. After Lily, he'd tried a few casual relationships, the *just friends* sort of thing, but those hadn't ended up any better than any other fucked-up relationship in his life. So he'd quit trying for a while and used *Escortè*.

There were similar services in other cities where he did the same thing. Kept it all nice and simple.

Then he hadn't had to worry about it for a while.

He'd met Selene. They clicked. They were compatible—in bed and out, and he hadn't had to mess with this shit.

Now? Starting all over again.

He tried not to feel aggravated. It was just a business thing. He paid for a date, had a woman with him for a few hours, spared himself the headache of dealing with some of the nightmares that came from being single at some of these parties. He also spared himself the nightmare that came from trying to have a friendly relationship that would just end in a disaster.

Really, this was for the best, right? All he had going with Selene was friendship anyway—granted, it was the friends with benefits sort of thing, but that could be found elsewhere.

Impersonal as hell. Yeah, that bothered him, and right now it was bothering him more than normal, but he'd finally found a way to balance his life and he didn't need anything rocking that boat.

You need to stop being so negative, he told himself. But it was damned hard considering every relationship he'd been in since high school had gone from hell to hella-bad in a blink.

"No." He threw the Porsche into park and climbed out, leaning against the side. "Not thinking about that." Part of the reason he hated coming back here. And that pissed him off. Chicago was *home*. It was home, and he avoided it like the plague except for rare visits home to see his sister, all because coming back here made him think of...

"And you're doing it again." Shoving away from the car, he pocketed the keys and headed toward his sister's office. It was quiet around here at night. During the day it was busy, but at night it was mostly vacant. Just a few random cars scattered in front of the other businesses. He recognized his sister's car, parked in front of the office, but he didn't see another one close to hers.

He didn't want to have to drive her home...that made it seem even more like a date.

A taxi, then. He'd get her into a damn taxi, or hell, Caleb would probably have cars there.

Yeah. He could get her into a car once the night was over with.

Then he'd head out to Blue's. Blue usually preferred that people wanting the...more *private* services contact her in advance, but she'd work something out. Distracted, thinking about that, he pushed through the door, thinking about maybe trying to put in a call to her before he even left Shera's. He needed to do something, right? He was edgy as hell and the only way to burn this kind of energy off was—

His brain just stopped.

He caught sight of the woman standing with her back to him and his mind came to screeching, crashing halt. All the blood in his head slowly started to sizzle and burn. A long, sleek back, displayed in a backless, pale dress, leaving lots and lots of sexy, smooth skin... His heart bumped once, hard, against his ribs, as his gaze dipped, lingering on the narrow curve of her waist, the round swell of her ass, and then onto long, sleek, sleek legs...

Ah, maybe he wouldn't be calling a car for her, after all.

Dragging his gaze up, he studied the back of her head and something started to click in the back of his mind. Dark hair, not quite black, shot through with lighter threads... His heart started to race. He knew this woman.

She turned around and he found himself staring into Chaili's blue eyes.

Marc had a fondness for her eyes. He didn't know why, exactly. Maybe it was because they were blue, and such a vivid blue they almost looked purple to his screwy eyesight. He didn't know why. Didn't care. He just knew she had amazing eyes.

It was a punch. A hard, brutal punch straight to his gut and he closed one hand into a fist as he continued to stare at her. Okay. She wasn't here for him. Chaili wasn't one of his sister's girls. She had something else going on... Then it occurred to him—Shera had absently mentioned setting up a line of male companions. Was Chaili...?

No.

Just. No. Even thinking about her paying some guy to take her out pissed him off.

What the fuck—

Shera appeared from the back office. "Hey, Marc." She had a smile on her face. An overly bright one. The kind of smile she'd always given him when she'd done something she shouldn't have and she wanted him to help keep her out of trouble with Mom. Except she was a grown woman.

Oh, shit.

Swinging his gaze back and forth between the two women, he lifted a brow and waited.

"Awesome news." Shera still had that wide, too-bright smile plastered across her face. "Chaili is going to keep you company tonight."

He was staring at her like she'd grown a second head.

Chaili felt like she might have.

Her heart raced and if he didn't say something, she was pretty sure she was going to start babbling like a fool. *No, you won't,* she told herself. He was here because he needed an intelligent, level-headed woman at his side for the night. Somebody who could carry a conversation *without* babbling, and that probably started now.

"Hello, Marc," she said, angling her head to the side. She could make polite small talk. She could do it, and do it well, even if it bored the hell out of her.

Something flashed in his golden eyes as he continued to study her.

So far, he still hadn't said a word. He prowled deeper into the office, looking oddly out of place. He came to stop a foot away from her, watching her with narrowed eyes, the gold in his eyes burning hot as he studied her face. "Just when did you start doing the companion thing, Chaili?"

She'd half-suspected he might ask. With a lazy shrug, she

answered, "It's fairly recent. I'm...picky, we'll say, about those Shera pairs me with. But I get tired sitting at home and well, you have to admit, this is an easy way to make money."

"So you're in it for the money."

Careful...careful... She knew he had more than a few people trying to get at his bank account. "Honestly, Marc, I told your sister I'd be happy to keep you company tonight without..." she waved a vague hand at the office and sighed, "...this. But your sister is something of a stickler about the rules. Since you came here, she's kind of adamant about doing it this way."

"Yes. I am." Shera came up and held out a hand, smiling at Marc. "You came in wanting a companion for the night. I'm providing the companion. Pay up."

The tense moment shattered and he scowled at his sister, reaching into his pocket. He shoved some bills into her hand and then looked at Chaili. "Shit, if I'd known you were up for going to stupid parties, I could have saved myself some money and the headache of dealing with Shera."

"Ahhh, but you're doing your part and investing in the local economy," Chaili said, smiling. She turned away and went to get her wrap and purse. Although she doubted she'd need the wrap, she'd rather have it than not. Before she could pick up the wrap, though, Marc was there and the fragile silk looked even more delicate in his hands. She swallowed and tore her gaze away from those long-fingered, agile hands. She'd always loved those hands...

Stop it, she told herself. He moved behind her and she closed her eyes, counted to ten.

As he draped the silk over her shoulders, she reminded herself she could handle this. That she'd *wanted* to handle this. It wasn't a date even, right? It was just a night. One night with Marc and then it was done. The one thing she'd always wanted...she could pretend for a night that he was hers.

"Chaili..." he murmured. The raw whiskey and velvet of his voice stroked over her senses like a caress and she had to fight not to shiver. "You look amazing."

Amazing didn't touch it.

Beautiful didn't quite touch it, either.

Marc was still trying to figure out the right way to describe it more than two hours later.

Something about her was...different.

He couldn't explain what, though.

Of course, it had been more than five years since he'd spent much time around her. She'd gotten serious with a guy. Married him for a little while. Then the marriage fell apart. He'd been out of the country when he'd heard they were splitting up, hearing the details from Shera.

When he'd emailed Chaili, all she'd told him in reply was, *We just weren't suited, Marc. It's not the end of the world.*

Not suited. Hell, he could have told her that. Tim Hardesty had been a fucking *ass*. He even knew the guy, in a roundabout sort of way, although he'd been careful to keep that connection very, very distant and Chaili, thank God, was blissfully unaware.

Frowning, he glanced over at her, studying her left hand. It was naked. She wore an odd ring on her right. It was some dark sort of metal, oxidized silver maybe, with a ruby in the middle, flanked by diamonds. Sometimes, he'd see her stroke it, in an offhand, absent manner that made him think it was habit.

She was chatting with the mayor, her voice rising, falling...open, friendly, and her smile was full of charm. He had absolutely no idea what they were talking about.

And he didn't care. Suddenly, he was jealous. He didn't want to share her with all the people in the crowd. He didn't want to be in the crowd, but that wasn't new. He was used to the crowds by now and after ten years of living this life, plus the ten years of struggling to get here, he knew he had to deal with it, but he didn't want to stand there while his "companion" did all the talking.

He wanted her talking to him.

This wasn't a fucking paid date.

"Excuse us," he said, cutting into the conversation. Giving the mayor and his wife a smile, he caught Chaili's hand in his and guided her through the crowd, out to where the party had spilled onto the terrace. Little lights had been threaded through the branches and lanterns floated through the pool. All around him, people were chattering and a few people drifted toward them—he ignored them. He just wanted a few minutes of peace and quiet with Chaili.

The gardens were likely the best place... Yeah. It was darker there, but quieter, and as they moved down one of the curved, winding paths, the voices started to grow more and more faint.

"Finally," he muttered.

From the corner of his eye, he saw Chaili slip him an amused glance, the lush curve of her mouth canting up. Damn it, that mouth. He'd noticed her mouth before...how could he not, but he was having a damned hard time keeping himself from staring at it nonstop tonight. It was slicked with something that stained it with a sinful shade of red and all he wanted to do was cup her face in his hands and taste that mouth.

Normally, he'd be inclined to do just that.

Except this was Chaili. He remembered the last time he'd tried that sort of thing with a friend. It had gotten all fucked up. Not that Chaili would ever do anything like that, but even aside from that, he didn't think it was a good idea to screw up a friendship just because he'd suddenly realized she was a gorgeous woman.

Well, no. He'd always known that.

And there'd been a time when he'd actually wanted to spend more time with this gorgeous woman. But it hadn't been doable and when he'd been back in town, she'd already been involved with Tim...

Shit.

"Are you okay?" Chaili asked softly.

"Stupid party," he said, shrugging his shoulders and pretending his problems rested solely on a dislike he knew she was familiar with. He'd never been much for socializing, a fact she knew well.

Chaili laughed softly, tipping her head back to the sky.

Moonlight shone down on her, gilding the hollows and curves of her face, her neck. Fuck, she was beautiful. She'd been pretty in high school, but now...

She looked over at him, a faint smile still on her lips. "You know, if you hate this so much, why go?"

"I'm supposed to." He shrugged. Spying a bench just ahead, he kept walking, still holding her hand. He didn't feel any desire to break that contact, either. As long as she didn't seem to mind.

"Well, Mom sometimes told me I was supposed to clean my plate, eat my lima beans and all that nasty stuff. I did it, but that doesn't mean it was good for me."

Chuckling, he sat down on the bench, straddling it so that

he'd be able to look at her without craning his neck around. "Well, sometimes this life is toxic, I think. My manager thinks it's a good idea to do this shit, but I mostly came because I know the guy throwing it, because it's a good cause and all. Caleb is...well...a friend. If it wasn't him, I would have ignored it." He shrugged it off, then focused on her. He was pretty damn certain he hadn't talked to Chaili for more than five minutes without Shera being around in years. And even then, Chaili was usually working. There were emails and sometimes he'd get to thinking of her and call, but the calls were sporadic and email, well, it just wasn't the same. "I don't see you much anymore."

"Well, it would be rather hard." She crossed her legs.

Marc managed not to stare at the long, sleek length for more than a second. *Yes, it's rather hard,* he thought absently. *Getting harder by the seco—*

He was ogling his sister's best friend. *His* friend. Chaili was his friend too. She'd been his friend for a damn long time. And it didn't matter, because his cock didn't care that this was a friend. Didn't care that he had this thing about fucking friends—that hadn't gone over well, right?

"After all, you kind of trot all over the world for about five months out of the year and when you're not trotting, you're holed up in New York working on another album. Once in a blue moon, you dash down here, but well..." She ended with a shrug. "Kind of hard for us to talk much or see each other when you're never in Chicago."

He tore his gaze away from her, staring off toward the house, blindly focused on the little lights in the trees. "I've been busy," he said gruffly. *I've been hiding.*

"Oh, I know. I'm proud of you." She tugged her hand, a subtle request that he let go, but he wasn't too inclined to listen to subtle. After a second, she stopped and he glanced over at her just in time to see her reaching up with her free hand. She stilled for the briefest moment and then continued, brushing his hair back from his face. "I always knew you'd make it, you know. You were so determined to do it, and you did."

He let go of the hand he'd been holding to catch her wrist, turning his face into her palm. The scent of her, something light and soft, had taunted him all night and he wanted to find the source of it, see if she'd dabbed it on her neck or between her breasts...it was just the slightest bit stronger on her wrist and he wanted to open his mouth, rake his teeth along her skin...

A weird scuffling noise caught his ears and just before he could do just what he'd been thinking about doing, a familiar voice rang out.

"Heya, Marc, buddy...where you at?"

Groaning, he closed his eyes.

Caleb...that was Caleb. They had an agreement, one they'd made a few years back after...well. After the disaster that shall be unnamed. Marc would come to Caleb's stupid-ass parties and Caleb, in turn, would keep his eye out for him.

And no doubt, that was probably what Caleb thought he was doing.

Lowering Chaili's hand, he gave her a tired smile. "That's my handler."

"You've got a handler?" she asked, quirking a brow at him.

"Sort of." He shrugged, glancing over as Caleb finally appeared around a bend.

"I never thought you'd be the kind of man who'd let somebody take you in hand, Marc," she teased, poking him in the knee.

He snorted. Unable to resist, he stroked a hand down her back. "Nobody wants that job, trust me."

"Hmmm. I know the feeling," she said, dipping her head. For a second, her shoulders slumped.

"Chaili?"

Rubbing his hand in a circle over the small of her back, he watched as she straightened and smiled up at him. "Some of us just aren't meant to be handled, I guess."

"There you are, man..." Caleb said, giving him an easy smile. But there was worry in his eyes. Worry, an apology.

Marc stood. Chaili did the same. "Hey, I don't think I introduced you two. Caleb, this is an old friend of mine." Slipping an arm around her waist, he tugged Chaili in closer, pressing a kiss to her brow. And because she was there, because he could, he let himself breathe in the scent of her... Aw, fuck, she smelled so damn good...

"Oh?" Caleb continued to stand there, watching them closely.

"Yeah." He wondered what she'd do if he...

"Marc." Caleb's voice, a hard, clear slap in the night, was an annoyance he could have done without.

Looking up, he shot his friend a dark look. "What?"

"You were telling me about your friend. An old friend. I remember a time you brought an old friend to one of my parties..." Caleb narrowed his eyes and said, "She was something of a bitch, really."

There were some weird undercurrents going on there and Chaili normally would have been A-okay leaving the two of them alone to hash it out, right up until Caleb tossed out the line about Marc's last *date*.

Easing away from Marc was almost like cutting off an arm. He felt so good against her and those hands, the hands she'd dreamed about stroking along her back, her neck, all those sensitive erogenous zones that made her want to shiver and sigh.

Shoving those needs to the side, she studied the man in front of her. He looked vaguely familiar. "Excuse me, did you just imply I'm a bitch?"

Behind her, she heard a muttered curse.

The man before her just smiled. "Not at all, Ms....?"

"Bennett. Chaili Bennett. I went to school with Marc. And you are...?"

"Chaili..." The man blinked. Glanced past her to study Marc. "Is this Shera's Chaili?"

"No. I'm my own Chaili," she interjected before Marc could respond. Turning around, she caught Marc's gaze. "I believe this gentlemen would like a word with you." She was rather torn, because she was *supposed* to stay at his side and keep the tramps and fans and groupies away from him. But she also didn't plan to stand there and be insulted. "Would you like me to wait for you at the entrance to the gardens?"

"No," Marc growled. Just the sound of his voice, gruffer than normal, had goose bumps breaking out over her flesh, and this time she couldn't suppress the shiver. He saw it and scowled. "You're cold."

She wasn't about to deny it, even though the temperature had nothing to do with her shivering. She couldn't exactly say, *Marc, your voice just turns me on, that's the problem.* "I'm fine," she hedged, ignoring the other man.

"We'll go inside...*after* I apologize for Caleb. I'm sorry, Chaili."

She rolled her eyes. "Why? You weren't the one calling me a bitch."

"No, he wasn't," Caleb said, moving closer, this time taking a position where she either had to look *at* him or turn her head. She met his gaze square on.

Chaili wasn't a short woman. In her bare feet, she was just a hair under five foot ten and with the heels she'd worn, she was right at six foot one. That put her eye to eye with this guy. She held his stare for a minute and then looked back at Marc. "You don't need to apologize for anybody, Marc."

"I do...if I'm the reason he's doing it," Marc said tiredly. He shot Caleb a sour look. "When I said he was my handler, I wasn't entirely joking. We've got an...arrangement, of sorts. I've had a few issues at these parties. He took it personally after one of them got ugly. He's just trying to make sure it doesn't happen again."

If Chaili hadn't had a few ideas just what sort of things Marc had dealt with, she might have asked. But she knew. She'd seen a few of them, back before he'd stopped coming home so much. Seeing the discomfort written on his face, she hooked her arm through his. "Don't worry about it, okay?"

"But I—"

"Chaili, I would like to apologize," Caleb said quietly.

She glanced over at him, met the direct gaze of his pale eyes. Sighing, she waved her hand. "Fine. Apology accepted."

He grinned at her, his teeth a white flash. "Now, I haven't exactly apologized...*yet*. I'm sorry, Chaili. I can't say I'm sorry for taking my...handling job so seriously, but I do know you're friends. Marc has mentioned your name. Often. I am sorry. If I'd known...well. That's not the point. I insulted you and I'm sorry."

"Accepted." She looked back at Marc. "Now can we go in?" She'd like to go back to where they had been, try to find that brief bit of magic they'd found. They'd used to be able to talk for hours. She could remember times when she'd listened to him

41

playing, practicing his music, working on new songs...she missed that. A lot.

"I'd rather stay out here," Marc said, shooting Caleb a look.

"You won't want to." No sooner had he said the words than a woman's soft, throaty contralto echoed through night. "I heard her talking about hunting you down. She wants you to play. A bunch of others are thinking it's a fine idea."

Marc groaned.

"Who is it?"

"A girl I dated for a while," he muttered. Not exactly an ex. He had that much sense, realizing she was bad news, but she'd been persistent and when she saw him earlier... He'd almost seen that maniacal gleam in her eyes again.

Caleb gestured to the right. "Head that way. Keep to the hedge. And not that I'm offering advice or anything, but if it were me, maybe what I'd do is go ahead and play. If you get to the piano and sit down before she finds you? You'll be surrounded by people before she gets back in there." Caleb flashed him another wicked grin. "Especially since I plan on telling her I saw you back around the pool house."

"And if I don't want to play?" Marc stared at him.

Caleb rolled his eyes. "You always want to play."

"He's got a point, Marc." Next to him, Chaili laughed and tugged on his wrist. "Come on. I haven't heard you play in ages. Maybe you could just pretend you're back at your old place, playing the way you used to."

Playing the way you used to...

Marc sat at the piano, stroked his fingers down the keys. It was a Fazioli. He'd played on them before, although he still preferred a Steinway. That had been the first piano he'd played on. It had been in middle school. When all his friends were playing the drums or a guitar, he'd been on an electric keyboard and then his mom had actually managed to find him that old upright Steinway at an estate sale, one she still kept at her place for him. He loved that piano.

He glanced up at Chaili to ask what she wanted him to play but she wasn't there. Scowling, he glanced around and saw that she was in the crowd. Holding out a hand, he waited until she sat down next to him. "What do you want me to play?" he asked, keeping his voice low.

If he was going to pretend he was playing the way he used to, for himself, for his friends, then he was doing just that.

She cocked her head and then smiled, leaned in. "'Walking in Memphis'."

"'Walking in Memphis'..." He hung his head, groaning. "Chaili, how many times have you made me sing that song? I was thinking about one of mine, you know."

She grinned at him. "Oh, that was just the first. I plan on making you sing 'True Believer' next."

"You and that song." Smiling, he laid his hands on the keys, closed his eyes. Whether it was his song or not...it was a magic one. Cohn, the singer and songwriter who'd written it had created pure gold with that one. Marc could understand why she loved it so much.

As he neared the end, he lifted his lashes, glanced over at Chaili. She was swaying, a strange little smile on her lips. As he came to the line...

And I sang with all my might...

He could hear her singing along with him. He might have asked her to sing louder, but he knew she wouldn't want to. She never did much care for that. Still, he liked listening to her.

43

He'd play again and have her sing with him when it was just them...then he realized he was thinking about spending more time with her.

A lot more...

The song ended and he made himself stop thinking, giving himself up to the music.

He did "True Believer" next, the song that had gotten him his big break. From there, he didn't bother asking, he just played. He forgot about the people around him. The only one who mattered was Chaili. From the corner of his eye, he glanced her way and his heart banged against his ribs as he realized she was watching his hands.

Seriously watching his hands. Almost the same way he'd been watching her mouth, he suspected. And there was a glassy little glint in her eyes—

Hunger burned in his gut, a terrible little knot that was taking on a life of its own.

He wanted Chaili. He'd managed to bash sexual hunger into submission over the past few years, letting it out in controlled, *very* controlled bursts, but this was...fuck.

This was gutting him.

A discordant chord filled the air and it jolted him back to reality. The song was nearly over anyway and he finished, pushed back and held out his hand to Chaili. They were leaving. He didn't know where they were going—he'd take her home if she insisted, but what he really wanted to do was take her to *his* place.

Take her there...and then take her, damn it.

Is this smart?

It was the calm, rational little voice in his head, the one he usually ignored.

This is Chaili...a friend. And not just any friend. She matters more than most...right?

Yes.

She did. It was almost enough to make him stop. Almost.

But the hunger inside him was a monster.

Chapter Three

Chaili couldn't even explain how she'd managed to get here.

Staring out over Lake Michigan, she swallowed the knot in her throat and tried to make herself breathe.

She shouldn't read anything into this.

Chaili knew that.

They'd had a nice night, talking. She'd gotten to spend a little bit of time with a man she'd loved for...always. Now he was just trying to...what? Unwind? She knew he hated those parties, knew he hated the crowds. Back in school, people had always thought he was borderline antisocial. She'd known better. People either frustrated him or just made him nervous. And now, so many of them expected things from him, expected him to be somebody he just wasn't.

That's what it was, she decided. He could be himself around her and that was why he'd brought her back here. That made sense, right? Yes. That explained—

"Here."

The rough, raw silk of his voice scraped over her senses and she all but whimpered as she turned around to face him. He held a glass of wine in his hand. She hesitated before reaching for it.

He grinned. "It's okay...you've got the same taste in syrup...um...I mean wine that my sister does. I bought it for her."

"Hey, it's not syrup." She took the glass and lifted it to her lips, took a small sip then sighed, smiling at the sweet, rather delightful taste. "Oh...that's good. What is it?"

"Elderberry mead. I found it at a winery a few hours from here when I was out driving around a while back."

"I like it. I need to see the bottle so I can go stockpile it." Not that she'd be able to drink much of it, but man...that was nice. She took another sip, closing her eyes and humming a little after she'd swallowed it. "I think the second taste is better than the first one."

"Let me try."

She opened her eyes and held the glass out to him. He took it, tried a sip and made a face. "It's not as bad as some. Come on." He continued to hold the glass as he caught her hand. "Grab the bottle, will you?"

"Where are we going?" she asked, trailing along behind him. The floor felt cool under her feet. She'd kicked off her shoes and the silk stockings she wore weren't much protection.

"I want to play some more." Over his shoulder, he glanced at her. "Is it okay?"

She arched a brow. "A private concert...with Mr. Marc Archer? You think I'm going to say *no*?"

"Smart ass."

The lights were off in the studio but he didn't bother to turn them on. She wished he'd turn them on, though...it was easier to pretend this all didn't feel terribly intimate. Terribly romantic...terribly seductive.

"Pour some more wine?" he said as they sat at the piano.

She swallowed, her throat dry...tight.

"Should I go get another glass?" she asked, pleased to hear that her voice wasn't shaking.

"No. We can share, right?" He took a sip and then laid his

47

hands on the keys of the piano.

Chaili closed her eyes and then muffled a groan as he went straight into "True Believer".

"Make a believer out of me..."

His words sank deep into her soul, wrapping around her and pulling her in. He was seducing her and he didn't even know it.

He could have kept on playing, just for her. Forever. He'd forgotten how amazing it was to do this. Playing for himself was always good. Playing for his fans...yeah, he loved that.

But there was something magic about sitting there in the dark and playing for her.

It was almost like he could talk to her through the music, and even though she said nothing back, he could hear her answer just in the way she moved, the way she smiled.

And it had always been like this, he realized.

Chaili seemed to find almost the same pleasure in the music that he did.

That same little smile bowed her pretty mouth up and she swayed, one hand curled around the wine glass, the other tapping out a rhythm on her thigh.

He had an image of catching the hem of her skirt. Pushing it up. Okay...*that* wasn't anything that had happened before tonight. But he had a feeling he'd be thinking hot and dirty thoughts about her for a long, long time after this. Hell, he was wondering why he hadn't done it before.

Closing his eyes, he tried to focus back on the music, but he couldn't block *her* out.

It was all there, twining through his mind. The raw, powerful vibe of the music. The song. The image of his hands on her thighs. Pushing that pretty skirt up. Catching the silken hose she wore and dragging them down, her panties...leaving her naked under that skirt. Then he'd play a little while longer. Just a little while, as he thought about her being naked under that elegant little white dress.

Get a grip, Marc. Or you're going to lose it before you even get started...

Get started. Was he actually thinking of trying to do this...

Hell, yes.

He must have lost his mind somewhere in the time he'd seen her standing in the office of *Escortè* and when he'd started playing for her back at the party, but he had every intention of having a taste of her. Just once, he thought. They were friends, right? They could have a night of nice, friendly sex and then go back to being friends...

Yes, because that had worked so well before.

Stop it, man. This isn't Lily. It won't happen that way. And if you can't get that through your head, you need to just take her home now, he told himself.

No. She wasn't Lily.

And he'd be damned if he took her home just yet. Unless that was what she wanted.

Clearing his throat, he took the glass of wine from her. "Ah...are you wanting to head home or you wanna hang around a while?"

She slid him a smile as she took the glass of wine back. "Hey, you played me one song. That does not a concert make."

Hot damn.

"'Walking in Memphis'?"

She just smiled.

He rolled into it, watching her a little closer this time. She

49

was looking at his hands again. Her face was flushed, although he didn't think it was the wine. He'd had as much as she and it was just the one bottle. Couldn't just be the wine, right?

She all but groaned as he launched into the one part that got to her, every damn time, right near the end.

His voice dropped, lower, rougher.

A shudder went through her and she grabbed the glass of wine, drank it down. They'd emptied the bottle and she wished she could blame the heat burning inside her on the wine, but it wasn't that. It was him. Always him—

"What is it about you and that song?"

As the music faded, she jerked her head up, saw him staring at her.

She tried to shrug. It wasn't the song, it was him. Something about the way he sang it, hell, the way he sang anything... She licked her lips and stared off into the distance, trying to figure out the right way to say something that wasn't a lie, but didn't leave her stripped bare.

A harsh groan reached her ears.

Startled, she looked at him, realized he was staring at her mouth.

Two seconds later, he was reaching for her.

Stunned, she couldn't think. As his lips covered hers, she just couldn't think.

Marc was kissing her.

Damn it.

Marc was kissing her—

Had she drank more wine than she'd thought?

"Open your mouth," he snarled against her lips, a harsh,

urgent command in his voice. "Give me your mouth."

Dazed, she did just that, opened for him.

His arms came around her as his tongue stroked across the bottom of her lip, slowly, seductively...teasingly. Oh, hell. She was in trouble. Big, big trouble...

And she didn't plan on doing anything to stop it, either. Not when he broke his mouth away to brush a line of stinging, hot kisses down her neck to her shoulder. Not when he stroked a hand up her thigh, the other cupping the back of her head.

Alarm, though, started to sound when he toyed with the fastening of her dress—alarm that would give way to terror if she let it.

Refusing to let that happen, she wiggled around until she was straddling his lap, her arms looped around his shoulders. Through the bodice of her dress, she felt the warmth of his breath, and when he pressed his mouth to her breastbone, she figured she needed to call a stop to this here and now. He didn't know and she just couldn't...

"Chaili...fuck, what have you got on under this skirt?"

She shivered as he spoke and Marc lifted his gaze, stared at her face, searching for some sign that he needed to pull back, but all he saw was the look of a woman wanting. Wanting *him*, damn it. Chaili wanted him.

This was insane and if he knew what was good for the both of them, he'd pull back, but they'd already opened Pandora's Box and he'd never be able to look at her again without remembering her taste. Without feeling the silk of her skin. Might as well ride the insanity to the end.

A slow grin canted up the corners of her lips. "You really want to know?"

"Fuck, yes."

Slowly, she eased back and then wiggled away. It wasn't necessary—the skirt was cut full and he could have pushed it up just fine on his own, but if she wanted to show him? Leaning back on his hands, he watched as she backed away a step or two from the bench.

"Just what's happening here, Marc?" she asked softly, her fingers toying with the hem of her skirt.

His lids drooped over his eyes as he stared at her fingers. Fuck, would she just let him see? "What do you think is happening here, Chaili?" he rasped.

"Well, I know what I *think* is happening here..." She eased the hem up and he caught a glimpse of lace, a few inches past mid-thigh.

His heart was going to stop. "You think maybe we should call it quits?" He looked away from her hands, met her gaze, those pretty jewel-like eyes, and waited.

"No." She shrugged and said, "I just..." She touched her tongue to her lips. "Call me shy. I'm not taking my dress off."

He blinked. Well, the night was young, he could work on that. "Does that mean I won't get to home base?" he teased, slipping off the bench and moving to stand next to her. He had to see what in the hell she had on under that skirt.

She laughed, a husky sound that went straight to his groin. "Oh, you can get to home base. Matter of fact, I'd rather you just skipped out on the whole third base bit too."

"But it's a lot of fun." He caught the hem of her skirt, dragged it up. "Just how shy are you, Chaili...do I get to see what's under here or not?"

She bumped him back, grinning. "I said I'd show you."

He obliged, taking a step away. Then another, because he

figured he'd see her better. And then he almost went to his knees as she dragged the skirt up, revealing the lacy tops of her stockings, the skinny straps of a garter.

"Turn around."

Her eyes widened a little and he could have kicked himself, but to his surprise she did it, still holding the skirt up, baring the stockings, her garters.

"Higher," he rasped.

A shudder raced through her and he narrowed his eyes, filing that little bit away. He'd think all of this through...later. Right now, he was having a hard time keeping his brain even functioning, and it only got worse as she tugged the skirt higher, higher, until it revealing the lacy edge of panties just a few shades darker than her skin. Lovely, just lovely...

Closing the distance between them, he gripped her waist and tugged her back against him, pressed his lips to her neck. She gasped and tilted her head to the side.

Raking his teeth along her skin, he slid his hand around, pressed it against her belly, splayed his fingers wide. As he cuddled his cock against her ass, he whispered, "Last chance, Chaili. Either we stop it now or we'll be sliding into home here very shortly."

"Well, not too shortly, I hope." She grinned at him over her shoulder.

Laughing softly, he slid his hand down, caught the hem of her skirt. Stroking his fingers along the lace of her stockings, he freed one strap. Another. Another. "I love your taste in lingerie," he whispered as he moved to the other leg. "I almost hate to undo these, but I really, really need you naked."

She chuckled. "They'll stay up."

"Yeah?"

Going to his knees after he'd freed the last strap, he stared at the round, taut curve of her ass. "Pull your skirt up again. Don't let go this time."

"You're bossy," she muttered.

Shit, she had no idea. But he noticed she didn't hesitate either, grabbing fistfuls of the full skirt, dragging higher, inch by scant inch. By the time the skirt had cleared the taut curve of her ass, he was about ready to shove it up himself, but he waited. Teeth gritted, muscles clenched...he waited. And sure enough, those lace-topped stockings still lovingly gloved her thighs, the straps of her garters hanging free. Reaching under the garter belt, he caught the panties and eased them down and dropped the pale, lacy scrap on the floor. Then, because she looked so damned hot, he hooked the garters back to her stockings as he leaned in, pressed his lips to the round curve of her ass.

She had the most amazing ass, he decided. Round, firm. She used to run in high school. Run, bike. She'd been the one of those brainiac athletic types. Judging by the long, sleek muscles, she was still into the active lifestyle.

Curving his hands over her ankles, he closed his eyes. He wanted to listen to every last shuddering sigh. Every catch of her breath as he touched her. As he tightened his hands just a little, her breathing hitched. When he stroked upward, that catch wasn't there.

When he stood and stroked the tips of his fingers along her spine, a soft moan escaped her. And when he touched his lips to her nape, she whispered his name.

But then, as he rested his hand on her waist, eased it around to her belly and stroked up, she tensed, every muscle in her body going tight. *Okay...* Another thing to file away. He stroked his hand back down, determined not to do a damn thing that would ruin this. Back to her neck, her spine...she really seemed to like that.

And he noticed when he caught one wrist in his hand, dragged it up over her head, a soft cry escaped and she sagged, her free hand coming up to slam against the wall as though she needed to brace herself.

Blood roared in his ears. Hungry, demanding—a beast that demanded to be let free, but he didn't listen. He just focused on her. Only her.

Sanity pushed its way in. Slowly. Surely. They needed to talk. Even if just for a minute. "Chaili, we need to...fuck..." Aw, hell. "That came out wrong. Damn straight, I need to fuck you, but I don't have anything here."

She tensed. Then relaxed. "Well...I'm on the pill. I know that doesn't cover everything, but I'm clean. Nobody since my divorce and I've had blood work done since then."

He pressed his head against her shoulder. "We're stupid doing this, you know that, right?"

"Does that mean you...?"

He pressed his lips to her shoulder. "Nothing to worry about here. I'm clean, although you damn well shouldn't trust that."

"Marc, if I can't trust you, who can I trust?"

She moved against him and those last threads of sanity snapped. Tightening his hold on her, he rasped against her ear, "Last chance, Chaili..."

"I think we passed that point already."

If he stopped, she just might die. Chaili was certain of it. But she'd wait until she killed him first. Just having him kiss her had been a shocking surprise, but then he...

Whoa.

Chaili wasn't much for being told what to do.

Unless it came to sex. She wouldn't ever call herself a true sexual submissive, but she definitely preferred to have her lover take the dominant position, and while she wasn't surprised that Marc was a little aggressive...this was blowing her mind.

This was something she had never guessed about him, hadn't ever even thought about, well...other than in her fantasies, but those were her fantasies, right? She could think whatever she wanted there.

This wasn't a fantasy.

This was really happening.

His hand tightened oh so slightly on her wrist and she shuddered.

Every inch of her hurt. Every inch of her ached. Every inch of her was tight with need and want and yearning.

When the raspy sound of his zipper sliced through the silence, she had to lock her knees just to keep upright. "I'm not waiting," he muttered.

Hell...he better not. She'd been waiting her entire life, it seemed.

He kicked her ankles apart and she bit her lip to keep from crying out. Damn it, he was killing her. She tugged tightly against the restraining hold he had on her wrist, but he didn't let go. That made her jerk harder and he squeezed tighter, stretched her hand higher, taking away some of her leverage as he leaned in. "Chaili...?"

"You should probably know that I'm thinking about the best way to kill you if you stop any damn thing you're doing."

"Anything, huh?" He stretched her hand higher, his thumb stroking in slow circles around her wrist.

Against her butt, she could feel him, the length of his cock, thick and hot, like a brand. Pushing back against him, she groaned. "Damn it, Marc..."

"Hey, I'm just doing what I was doing...in the name of self-defense."

"Would you just fuck me?" she snarled.

And then she cried out as he caught her around the waist and lifted her. She felt him between her thighs, probing, pushing... Her head fell back against his shoulder and she cried out.

The room shifted sideways—no. Wait. That was just them—he'd moved. She felt the floor under her knees, felt him at her back and then she groaned as he pushed against her. As he slowly sank inside, deep, deeper, she shuddered and twisted her hips, gripping him with her inner muscles, shuddering as he stroked over every sensitive, aching nerve ending, hitting all those *right* spots...and a few she didn't even know she had. Then he started to retreat and she clenched down in a desperate hope to keep him inside her. *No, not yet...*

"Aw, fuck," he growled, surging back inside. Deeper. Harder.

Again. Again.

She moved back to meet him each time, twisting her hips, clasping him tight and milking him, desperate for the feel of him inside her.

"Stop it," he growled, pressing the flat of his hand against the small of her back. "What's your hurry?"

She couldn't even think to *understand* the question, much less *answer* it.

Too long...Marc... Afraid of what she might let herself say if she said anything, she bit her lip, once more clenched down around him—every last nerve ending sizzling as his cock sliced through her pussy, each stroke going deeper, hotter...taking her deeper, hotter. And despite her determination not to talk, she found herself keening out his name.

"That's it," he muttered behind her. "Come for me, Chaili... Fuck, you're beautiful..."

And for a little while, she even believed it again.

"Say you'll stay the night."

Nearly thirty minutes had passed and he'd moved only once, to shift around and sit with his back against the wall and pull her into his lap. She felt just about perfect there.

Everything was just about perfect. She was soft and warm in his arms, snuggling against him with her cheek on his shoulder and every now and then she'd make this soft, kittenish little sigh that had his heart twisting. And she was stroking her fingers across his chest. Lightly. But it was like she couldn't stop touching him, and he really liked that.

He didn't want to stop touching her, either.

He was rather certain this had been the best sexual experience of his life.

With Chaili.

He'd lost his mind a little bit there, grabbing her wrist that way, pushing her against the wall. And she'd responded like... His lids drooped, an unconscious smile curling his lips as he recalled just how she'd responded. Perfectly.

Yeah.

Everything was just about perfect.

But it was getting late, he was tired and if he wanted to make love to her again, he'd best go ahead and talk her into staying. And she hadn't said anything. Turning his face into her hair, he said softly, "I want you to stay the night. Say you will."

She sighed and stroked her hand down the front of his shirt. "Is that really a good idea?"

Tangling his fingers in her hair, he tugged her head back, staring down into her eyes. "At this point, what can it hurt?"

"Hmmm. Well, put like that..."

Stroking his hand up the sleek length of her thigh, he said, "You should know I plan on getting the two of us in the shower. Then I plan on getting us in my bed where I can lay you down and take my time with you." He cupped her in his hand and stroked his finger around her entrance, watched as she shuddered. "I never did get to taste you."

"Hmmm." Her lashes drooped. "That all sounds lovely...but..."

"But?" Fuck. What...

"Maybe I could take a shower by myself." She darted a look at him, jerked one shoulder in a half shrug. "I told you. I'm..."

"Shy." Laughing a little, he slid his hand out from under her skirt and eased her off his lap. Once he got to his feet, he helped her up. "Okay, you head on upstairs...my room is at the end of the hall, on the right. Bathroom is straight on through. You've got fifteen minutes and I'm not coming up until the time is up, because I've got a thing for naked women."

Chapter Four

Chaili found a shirt hanging off the foot of the bed and grabbed it.

In the shower, she scrubbed off with his soap, washed her hair with his shampoo, and shuddered as she realized she'd leave here smelling of him in so many ways.

She was done in under eight minutes and that left her with too many minutes to dry her short hair and stare at her reflection.

At her scarred reflection.

She could just show him, she supposed.

But she didn't see the point.

This wasn't going to last once morning was over. Marc traveled all over the world and was in Chicago once in a blue moon. She didn't see him often and over the past few years it was even less frequent than normal.

It was almost like he avoided Chicago anymore.

This was a once-in-a-lifetime chance to catch a dream and she was going to run with it, enjoy every second of it while it lasted. Closing her eyes, she started to button the shirt, hiding away the scars.

In a few more hours, she'd leave.

Like Cinderella, and the magic of this very strange night would end...and maybe she wouldn't have her glass slipper but she could have the memories.

With that in mind, she squared her shoulders and stared at

her reflection. She'd wanted to spend a night with him. Just talking. Maybe it was kind of lame. Yeah, it was. But...

"Stop it," she whispered. She wanted a night. One brief, fun night, something she'd done on a whim and, damn, had she gotten her night. And more.

She even felt...whole, in some ways. Some part of her felt *real* again. She felt *wanted*—she hadn't felt that way in years.

He took longer than fifteen minutes.

It took that long just to get his head on straight.

Of course, when he walked into his room and saw her standing at the floor-to-ceiling windows, staring out over the lake, wearing one of his shirts, he had to stop and catch his breath.

"What is it about a woman wearing a guy's shirt?"

She startled and turned around, stared at him. She looked puzzled and then glanced down, stared at the black dress shirt, shrugged. "Sorry. I wasn't exactly planning on spending the night and I figured you didn't keep pajamas on hand for guests." She bit her lip, tugging at the collar. "I can use a T-shirt or something."

He shook his head, staring at her. "I think I might have the shirt bronzed or something. I'll never be able to wear it without thinking about how you looked in it."

"Whatever," she snorted, rolling her eyes before turning back to stare out over the lake. "You must like the water. I never realized you were that into the lake."

"I'm not." He came up behind her, stroked a hand down her spine, watched as she shivered. So fucking responsive...it was almost painfully erotic, just to watch how she reacted when he

61

touched her. "I just like the privacy. I told the realtor to find me a quiet place, someplace well outside the city and this was one she showed me. When I saw the house...well, it was just mine."

"Hmmm."

Resting one hand on the base of her spine, he stroked, easing the shirt up. In the glass, he could see just the faintest outline of her face, watched as her lashes dipped. *Mine...*he thought. It was a rather dizzying surprise to look at her and realize he felt a strong, stunning possessiveness.

This was weird. Deeper than anything he'd felt. Different. He wanted to spend a hell of lot more time with Chaili than just one night.

Something he'd think about in the morning.

One of many things he needed to process.

Something he'd have to take his time on and think through, because Marc was damn good at screwing things up when he didn't think them through.

"Come to bed," he whispered against her ear.

"Aren't you going to shower?"

Groaning, he dropped his head against her shoulder. "Damn. I knew I was forgetting something."

Chaili chuckled, turning around and pressing her lips to his neck. "Well, the shower was your idea. I'm just fine with going to bed now." She paused and then took a deep breath. "Marc...you smell like me. I kind of like it."

He wrapped his arm around her, hauling her against him. "You've got my shirt on..." He buried his face against her neck and breathed in the faint scent of his own soap on her skin. "And I can smell my soap on you. It's never been that fucking sexy on me. I swear, I could eat you alive."

A shudder wracked her. "Ah, I've got no problem with that.

Not one."

Killing me, he thought. He kept his head buried against her neck for a minute, waited for the racing of his heart to stop.

The bed cradled her like a damned cloud and if she'd been lying on it at any other time, she just might have closed her eyes, sighed in sweet bliss. But just then, as Marc laid her down, tugged her to the edge, she was having a hard time doing much of anything but reaching for him.

He caught her wrists and pushed them back to the bed.

Groaning, she fisted her hands in the sheets—cool, silky sheets that felt as smooth as satin against her skin. He caught her hips and dragged her to the edge of the bed, her legs hanging over where he knelt between her thighs. "I think I'm going to have that taste of you now," he rasped, draping her legs over his shoulders. "But I don't want you coming yet."

Staring at him through her lashes, she licked her lips—her mouth was so dry. Looking at him had a way of doing that to her, but now...? "I'm about to come just *looking* at you."

"Don't." He closed one hand around her ankle, guiding her leg up until her heel was pressed against her ass.

As his dark head bent down, Chaili closed her eyes and cried out. Need was a painful whip, lashing against her. His tongue rasped against her clit, circled, teased...dipped lower.

He pushed inside and she could feel the climax rushing up. Swearing, she clutched at the sheets, arching off the bed. She stared at his bent head, but that didn't help. *Don't come...I can't...can't come yet—*

"You're close to coming," he whispered, lifting his head and watching her from under heavy-lidded lashes. "I don't want you coming yet."

"I won't," she panted. "Just don't stop."

Fuck, she was beautiful.

Face flushed, a sexy little snarl on her lips as she glared at him... It made him hotter than he thought was possible. "Hmmm..." Dipping his head, he stroked his tongue around her clit, teased the hard little bud with his teeth. At the same time, he pushed a finger inside her, screwing his wrist. "You sure of that?"

Her head fell back, exposing the elegant line of her throat as she shuddered, moaned. "Damn it. Yes. I'm sure..." And as she spoke, she twisted her hips and started to rock against him.

"Be still." He rested one hand against her belly, watching her.

Her body tensed, but she stilled, her head still hanging back. He could hear the ragged rhythm of her breathing. Fuck, he wanted to see her naked. Shifting around, he reached for the placket of buttons, but the second he did, she tensed, scrambling around and sitting up.

"No." She hunched her shoulders in.

"Chaili..." He eased in, leaning in to kiss her.

She stilled, opening her mouth for him, but when he reached for the front of her shirt again, she twisted away. "I said *no*," she snapped.

Narrowing his eyes, he said flatly, "I want you naked."

He'd already noticed that while she was cocky as all get out about it, when he gave her an order...she followed it. But this time, she remained there, hunched, those proud shoulders slumped. "I said *no*, Marc." She shook her head and squirmed away.

As she went to stand, he rose and caught her wrist, kept her from walking away.

"Okay." Lifting her wrist to his mouth, he murmured against her skin, "I don't get why, but okay."

Her throat worked as she swallowed and in the depths of her eyes he saw a glimpse of something that made him want to scream. Made him want to break something. Tear something apart.

Stark, naked pain.

"I can't take it off, Marc," she said quietly. "Don't try again, okay?"

Nodding, he pulled her against him. "Okay." He wasn't about to lie and say he understood, and one thing was damn clear...the next time they were together, he wasn't going to back off quite so easily. And there was going to be a next time, if he had anything to say about it. And another. Another.

But for now...

Catching her hands, he lifted them to his shirt. "Take off mine, then," he told her.

They said nothing else as she stripped away his shirt, although she left it hanging open as she undid his belt, unbuttoned his trousers. Then she went to push his shirt off his shoulders and her breath hitched in her throat. White teeth caught the swell of her lip as she reached up and touched the silver hoop he had through his right nipple. Her pupils spiked and she swayed closer.

"I'm still dressed," he rasped, reaching up and fisting his hand in the hair at the nape of her neck.

She closed her eyes, shuddered. Her shoulders rose, fell, and then she lifted her lashes, stared him in the eye as she finished pushing his shirt off. As she did, though, she leaned in, caught his nipple in her mouth, tugging on the hoop. Heat hurtled through him, straight from where her mouth touched to his balls. As she went to her knees in front of him, her hands catching the waistband of his trousers and the boxer briefs he wore, Marc sucked in a ragged breath.

Staring at her, on her knees in front of him, the black shirt she wore still hiding too much of her from him, he helped kick the rest of his clothes away and stood there, waiting to see what she'd do.

She just stayed there.

Slowly, he reached out, closed his hand around the aching flesh of his cock, stroked. Her breath caught. "Look at me," he ordered.

She tipped her head, her eyes darting from his face to his cock. Each time her gaze dropped, it lingered longer. Longer. He continued to stroke himself, watching her face, and when she licked her lips, he swore, pressed his thumb to the lower one. "I want your mouth on me."

Chaili shuddered and lifted herself higher, her mouth open.

Aw...his eyes closed at the first touch. There was no hesitation in her, no shyness. As she swayed against him, soft little humming sounds vibrated out of her throat and even *that* was a brutal pleasure against his senses. Fisting his hands in her hair, he cupped her head, opened his eyes to watch her.

Her mouth stretched open wide to take him, deep...then shallow.

And she was watching him. Shooting looks up at him every now and then, as though she just had to see how she was affecting him. The muscles in his thighs tensed and his balls were on fire—but he wasn't going to come. Not yet. This was too fucking good—

Snarling, he caught her hair in his hand, stilling her

movements. "Get up," he ordered, but he didn't wait. He caught her arms, dragged her up against him and tumbled them both back onto the bed, shoving that stupid shirt up to her waist. "Ride me. I want to watch you this time."

Should have turned on the damn lights.

The dim glow coming in from the bathroom, the hallway, just wasn't enough, and although the moon was full, the silvery light that fell in to gild her skin and hair wasn't enough, either.

He wanted to see all of her, and he wanted to see her in the full, bright light, learn every last curve of her. Learn every last taste. Every nuance and sigh...

But for now, this was pretty damn excellent he decided as she lifted up and closed her hand around him, guiding the head of his cock to her gate. Hot and tight, she closed around him like a glove, sinking down on him slower, slower... Oh, so perfect...

"Chaili," he rasped.

She shuddered, her eyes going wide before drifting closed, a fey little smile dancing on her lips. He wanted to see her eyes, wanted her watching him as he watched her, but in that moment...

As she rocked against him, taking him deeper and deeper, he just stared. Etching it on his memory.

A dream...made real.

That's what this was.

As he arched beneath her and groaned, his cock swelling inside her, she had to open her eyes, had to watch him. Just to see that this was real. And it hit her, grabbed her around the throat to see those tawny eyes watching her.

He reached up, touched her mouth, stroked down, down,

down... She tensed, but all he did was stroke his fingers down along the middle of her torso, along her belly, until he could circle his thumb around her clit. One circle. Two. "I want to see you come," he rasped.

She'd been holding it back...

Now, she leaned forward, her hands braced on his shoulders. His hands curved on her hips, fingers digging into her ass. "Marc," she whimpered. Then she had to bite her lip, because she almost said it. Almost...

"Let me see you come, Chaili."

It had been building inside, a storm she'd been holding back and now, she gave into it. As it broke inside her, she kept her teeth locked on her lip, biting so hard she tasted blood.

And in her mind, she said the words she'd wanted to say to him for so long.

I love you...

Morning came, a brilliant golden glow. Beautiful, stunning...and too damned early.

Groaning, Chaili snuggled deeper into the bed, trying to hide from the light and wondering why in the hell she'd left her curtains open. She didn't want to get up to shut them, though. She never slept this well anymore. Her mattress was ten years old and there was this one spot where she always ended up with the wires poking into her ribs—

"I take it you're not a morning person."

She tensed.

Oh, hell.

Either she was still dreaming or the dream she'd been having last night...

The warm male body pressed up against her back shifted, stretched. A hand, big, hard and warm, caught her leg just behind the knee, pushed it high. "I'm going to fuck you again, Chaili," Marc whispered against her ear. "Just like this."

"Oh, hell."

He laughed softly as he moved up onto his knees.

She'd barely caught her breath before he pushed inside, crouched over her. Her left leg was trapped between his and he had her right leg hooked over his elbow. As he started to thrust inside her, her breath caught.

The black silk of his hair fell into his face, and his eyes, still heavy lidded with sleep, watched her.

"I want to do this again," he rasped as he moved over her, in her, possessing her. Overwhelming her. "And again. And again."

In the soft, golden light of morning, there was no mistaking the want in his eyes. The need.

And she feared it would be hard to hide what *she* felt. Closing her eyes, she turned her face to the pillow as he moved inside. Bit her lip as her heart swelled inside her, as the need and yearning and want threatened to spill out and overwhelm her.

*Love you...*she thought blindly. Desperately.

Always him. Only him.

And now, not only did she have her dreams and memories to haunt her, she had the taste of him imprinted on her senses, the feel of his hands rasping over her flesh...

"Look at me," he growled.

Turning her head, she stared at him through her lashes. Fire burned through her. And at the look in his eyes, the need only grew.

"Watch me."

Her breath caught as their gazes locked. The jewel-like tones of her eyes seemed to glow. Seemed to burn.

Marc hunkered over her, wishing he could make the moment last...and last. She was so fucking beautiful, and when she looked at him, he felt...hell, like himself. He felt real and whole, like he didn't have to hide, like she was just fine with the man making love to her.

But it couldn't last...wouldn't. As she tightened around him, her lashes drifting low over her eyes and a broken moan escaping her, the silken muscles in her pussy milked him, clutching at him. She was so soft, so tight. She reached down, gripping his wrist, her nails sinking into his skin like she had to have *something* to hold on to.

He understood that... He felt like he was about to fly into a million pieces.

As she cried out, the climax twisting through her, he drove deep...and fell apart.

He wasn't even sure if there were a million pieces left when it ended. She just might have undone him completely.

He was cuddled up against her back once more and Marc was pretty certain it was the best way to spend a morning. Ever. Normally he'd think something like that through about fifty times before he said it to a woman, and maybe debate about it for a few days, wait until the opportunity arose again before he said it. Especially considering how often his mouth ended up getting him in trouble.

But he didn't have to do that here, not with Chaili. Stroking his thumb along her side, he reminded himself of that.

Then his thoughts stuttered to a halt as he stroked his thumb over her side. There was a ridge under his thumb. Raised against her soft, smooth flesh. A scar...?

What...

As his mind started to process that, she reached up with her hand, guided his hand down to her hip. Closing his eyes, he blew out a breath. She had a scar on her ribs. Okay. Would explain why she didn't want to take off the shirt. He'd thought maybe she was just self-conscious. Chaili had always had a long, lean build. Amazing legs. An ass that made his hands itch to touch... Jerking his mind back on track, he thought it through. So it was self-consciousness. And maybe something else. He could still remember that flicker of pain he'd seen in her eyes last night. He'd figure it out.

It was a bridge he'd cross next time, or the time after.

Now he just needed to make sure she'd be open to a next time.

"I've been thinking," he said softly.

Chaili laughed, shooting him a look over her shoulder. "Thinking...is that what we call it now?"

He swatted her hip lightly. "Brat." He nipped her neck and then licked her skin, loving the taste of her. "Hmmm, you taste good. Anyway, I was thinking. I've decided this is probably the best way I've ever spent a morning. Matter of fact, I'm pretty damn sure of it."

A faint blush settled over her cheeks. "Hmm. Well, considering it's a ridiculously early hour, I guess it's not been too bad."

"Gee, thanks," he said deprecatingly.

"Hey, I can't help that you've got windows that face the sun and I was wakened at the crack of dawn." She sniffed and snuggled back down into the bed. "Although I guess it's a good thing. I've got a big project and I need to get to work. If something didn't wake me up, I just might have slept the day away. This bed is amazing."

He grinned down at her. "So you're pleased about the bed."

A smile curled her lips. "I'm pleased about everything right now, truth be told."

"Good." He sat up, pushing his fingers through her hair. "I was wondering...ah, maybe we could go out sometime. Like, um...a date. You know."

Smooth, Casanova, he told himself.

She rolled onto her back, pulling the blankets up and tucking them under her arms. "A date."

"Well...yeah." Shooting for a smile, he managed what he figured wasn't *too* strained. And why did he have to try and smile around Chaili, anyway? Being with her felt easy. Natural. Why in the hell was he putting up with women who annoyed the hell out of him when he could have this? "I mean, we had fun and all, right?"

"Sure." She sat up. "Fun. Although this was a little more than I think we planned on."

"Yeah." Okay, he was struggling here. He knew it, could feel it. Could feel the slippery ground under his feet. "I guess I got my money's worth, right?" As soon as he said it, he wanted to jerk it back. "Shit. I didn't mean it like that."

She gave him a brittle smile. "Of course."

As she rose from the bed, he scrambled forward, reaching for her hand.

"Damn it, Chaili, wait!"

"I really have to get going." She glanced around, crossed the room to pick up the dress she'd draped over a chair in the sitting area by the northern wall. "That project of mine has a deadline coming up. If I don't get some time put in every day, I won't get it done and I can't afford to lose an account like this."

"Chaili..."

With a vague smile on her face, she crossed to stand in front of him, rising on her toes to kiss his cheek. "It was a nice night. I hope I did okay at the party. The companion thing is a still fairly new for me."

His money's worth.

Chaili would like to tell him to shove the money up his very fine ass, but she wasn't about to let him know just how much he'd hurt her. As she finished zipping up her dress, he knocked on the door. "Damn it, Chaili, will you get out here and talk to me?"

"Sure. Just give me a minute," she called out, forcing her voice to sound a hell of a lot easier than she felt. She wanted to chew glass. Wanted to cry. Wanted to hit something. Wanted to break. She didn't know what she needed, but she needed something.

Well, no, that wasn't true. She needed to get the hell out of there and now. Turning on the water, she splashed it on her face, hissing at the cold shock of it. She finished washing her face and scrounged around for a toothbrush, but he only had his and she wasn't about to touch it. She had one of those disposable ones in her purse; it would do the trick. She'd grab some of the mouthwash, though.

In another minute, she was about as ready as she was going to be and she opened the door to see him standing there. Armed with a polite, professional smile, she lifted a brow and asked, "What did you need to talk about? We need to make it fast, though...I really do need to get going."

"Chaili..." He just stared at her, his eyes locked on her face.

Silence stretched out. Forcing herself to keep smiling, she checked the time on the big wall clock and then looked back at him. "Mark, I have to get moving. Did you want to drive me back or should I call a cab?"

"You're not calling a fucking cab," he growled. "It would take forever to get here and you live a good thirty minutes away."

"That's fine. Can we talk on the drive back, then?" She headed out of the room. Out of the corner of her eye, she saw him scrub his hands over his face.

If she didn't have a gaping, bleeding wound in her heart, she might have taken some pity on him. But she just couldn't. Not right now. Not yet.

Maybe after she'd had a few weeks, a few months...a few decades...to lick her wounds. She shouldn't have tried, damn it. Not after the last time. She should have known better.

Her purse was in the kitchen and she scooped it up, dug out one of those mini toothbrushes she'd tossed inside and turned around, found Marc standing just a few feet behind her, a silent, brooding shadow. "Just a minute," she said, flashing him another polite, easy smile. *That's it,* she told herself. *Keep it nice and professional. Like you should have done yesterday. It will be done soon and you can forget this ever happened*—liar!

Not that she would be able to forget. And damn it, anyway. Why did he have to say that...

Locked inside the bathroom off the main hallway, she pressed her back against the door and sullenly tore the foil off the back of the toothbrush packet. She'd had some seriously good memories stockpiled there. A lot of them. And now...

Tears pricked the inside of her eyelids. Now this was just going to be another one of the hollow, empty aches that kept her awake at night.

Chapter Five

She wouldn't talk. Oh, hell, she talked, but she commented about how pretty a morning it was. What a nice drive it was. How nice the party had been.

And every *single damn time* he tried to circle back around to what had happened, she waved it off. Smiled vaguely. Acted like she didn't comprehend what he was talking about.

As they got closer to Shera's place in Arlington Heights, he wove through the traffic, wishing it were actually *worse* for a change. He was running out of time to get her to talk to him, to get her to forgive him for being an ass. "Listen, Chaili, I was an asshole this morning. I didn't mean that the way it sounded, okay?"

Ha. He actually got the entire sentence out—

"Hmm?"

Shooting her a look, he realized she was messing with her iPhone. What the... Snarling, he reached over and snagged the phone, shoved it between his legs.

"Hey!" she snapped.

"You're welcome to get it," he offered.

She sighed. "Marc, I'm trying to take care of some business here, okay?"

"And I'm trying to talk to you. I told you I was sorry. I keep trying to tell you." Shooting a look in the rearview mirror, he cut over for the exit and shot onto the ramp.

"You're going the wrong way. It's the next exit."

"I'm taking the long way around," he said. She was finally talking—or at least not changing the subject. "I'm sorry, Chaili."

"Yes. You've said that. Repeatedly. You're sorry. I heard you. It's not an issue." She paused, held out a hand. "Can I have my phone?"

"I told you...you're welcome to get it." He slowed down at the red light and looked over at her.

She had her head averted, staring out the window.

Hell.

"Can we...?" Shit. He was fucking this up every which way he turned. "I want to see you again."

"You see me fairly often, Marc. Or at least you do when you're in town." She gave him a tired smile. "And hey, I live with Shera...that's not likely to change any time soon."

"Are you deliberately being obtuse here or is it just me?"

Her answer was interrupted as somebody behind him laid on the horn. Marc jerked his gaze up and glared into the rearview mirror, not that it made him feel better.

"I'm not being obtuse and I'm sorry if I'm being difficult," she said, shifting in the seat. She plucked at the hem of her skirt, smoothed it down over pretty, tanned thighs. "Last night was a business arrangement, remember? I don't do the companion thing often and I probably won't be doing it much longer, so..."

"I'm not talking about a fucking companion," he snarled, whipping the car off the road and arrowing into the parking lot of a nearby shopping center. "I'm talking about you and me. On a fucking date. Is that so hard to comprehend?"

She turned her head. Just stared at him.

"Well?" he demanded. "Are you going to give me an answer?"

A slow smile bowed up her lips. "Sure, Marc. I'll give you an answer...after you give me my phone."

"Aw, shit." Shoving a hand through his hair, he grabbed her phone and dumped it into her hand. "You're going to say no, aren't you?"

"Damn straight." She jerked open the door and climbed out. "Take it easy, baby."

"Oh, no, you don't." He pushed his door open, pausing just long enough to grab a pair of sunglasses and a hat before jogging to catch up with her. She moved awful damn fast considering she had on a pair of toothpick heels. "Wait a minute."

"Leave me alone. Last night is over."

He caught her arm and jerked her to a stop and then groaned as she stumbled in her heels. Steadying her, he reached up to touch her cheek and it was a blow to the heart when she turned away, averting her face before he could make contact. "Hell, Chaili, you know what an asshole I can be when I don't think through every fucking thing that comes out of my mouth," he whispered. "You used to tease me about it all the time..."

"Yeah." She nodded. "I know. Like I said, it's not an issue. Over and done. Now let me go."

"Let me take you home."

"No. I'll call a cab or walk. It's not far. I need some air anyway."

"I want to drive you home," he said. Hell, he was edging too damn far into desperation territory here, but there wasn't much he could do about it. He *was* desperate. Ready to beg, if he had to.

"I already said *no*." Her voice was flat, firm. And when she tipped her head back to glare at him, there was a harsh glint in her eyes. "And if you don't let me go right now, you're going to be very, very sorry."

"I'm not ready to let you go..." Hell. He'd just discovered this part of himself. Of *them* and she wanted him to walk away because he was an asshole?

Her eyes flicked over to the side and her mouth curved. "Think it through, Marc. I'm getting ready to piss you off so bad."

Narrowing his eyes, he glanced over.

Awww. Shit. There was a news truck parked less than thirty feet away. In front of one of the local music stores too. She wouldn't. Okay, maybe she would. But there was a chance nobody would notice, right? "Chaili..."

"One."

"You're being..." Snapping his mouth shut, he bit back anything he could say that would make things any worse than he'd already made them. "Can we maybe just rewind things? Go back to before we woke up? *Please?*"

"Two."

Letting his hand fall away from her arm, he backed away a step. "This isn't done, damn it. I get it...you're mad at me. I know you well enough to know that."

"No, you don't," she whispered, lowering her head.

Finally, she looked back at him and for a moment he saw something other than that blank, smiling mask she'd been showing him all damned morning. It was the pain he'd glimpsed in her eyes. Right after he'd fucked things up. "If you knew me all that well, you'd know I'm not pissed." Her gaze roamed over his face and she went to turn away.

His heart stuttered and then stopped beating when she

paused, whirled back around and came up to him, cupped the back of his head. As her lips crushed to his, he went to grab her.

But she was gone in the next breath, striding down the sidewalk, and she didn't look back.

Chaili hadn't been lying about the project she needed to get done.

It was a major one, and the deadline was two weeks away. But she'd get it done within another two or three days. So she didn't go home and get right to work.

She'd planned on it.

But when she let herself into the little apartment above Shera's garage, adamantly telling herself, *I won't cry, I won't cry, I won't cry*...she saw the check. Her share of the money from her *companion appointment*. That was how Shera liked to label them. Kept it all nice and impersonal.

Four hundred dollars—her cut from the thousand Shera had received. Four hundred bucks for what was supposed to be a few hours at a party. Not bad. Not that Chaili had even wanted the damn money anyway, but now she felt nauseated.

Ignoring the check, she stalked into her bedroom, jerked off the dress and kicked it and the heels into a corner. Her feet were *killing* her—walking had been just plain stupid and it was close to three miles from the point where Marc had pulled off the interstate. She'd ended up calling a cab but not soon enough. Her feet felt like somebody had pulverized every last bone.

Wiggling into a pair of slim black jeans, she tugged on a loose, cowl-necked shirt and slid on a pair of her nicer sandals. The things were old. Most of her nice stuff was. She couldn't afford the good stuff anymore, but that was okay. Sooner or later, she liked to tell herself. Sooner or later...

Once she'd changed, she stormed back into the kitchen, shoved the check into her pocket and dug up the keys to the car Shera let her use. Shera had two of them. One year, Marc had given her a sporty little Roadster for a Christmas present, so the practical SUV Shera had paid off mostly sat unused. Chaili knew the truth of it, although Shera would deny it.

Shera kept it around so Chaili could use it, and it was a scrape on Chaili's pride too. There were so many of them over the past few years, so damn many.

But this wouldn't be.

It took thirty minutes to get to *Escortè* and she made the entire drive dry-eyed and clearheaded. She'd known what she was getting into when she insisted on doing the date with him. Maybe she should have pushed harder. Insisted that she not sign the fucking contract, or maybe even just called Marc, told him she'd like to go out with him.

She'd known what she was getting into—she'd signed that damn contract. And maybe it had been laid out to protect him, but it had screwed her. She should have realized how he'd perceive it and argued harder, or just said screw it.

Now it was done and even if he tried to insist he didn't mean it as he'd said it, it was still an ugly, awful wound inside her. One she'd have to come to grips with, somehow.

First, though. This.

Get through this, go home. Maybe get drunk. Cry in a hot tub of water. Sleep it off. And tomorrow, she'd get back to real life. Hell, if she could afford it, she'd take a few days off...

Wait a minute.

The cabin.

Gina had been inviting her up to the cabin. One of the

designers she knew had a cabin about an hour away from Chicago and was always inviting Chaili to come up there when she decided to head out. If she remembered right, she'd seen a tweet from Gina about heading up to her place...

Yeah. She was going to see if Gina was up there. And if so? She'd go crash with a friend for a few days. Lick her wounds. She could still work up there, do what she needed to do. And get away.

Sounded like a plan.

With that in mind, she shoved through the door to *Escortè*. Shera was there, in the client seating area, going over a file with Brienne, one of the office assistants.

They kept a skeleton staff on weekends, usually one of the assistants and a *personal companion specialist*—another of Shera's labels. But there were only two of the "specialists". Shera and Deana. And Deana was out on maternity leave so Shera was working a lot of extra time lately.

Shooting Brienne a quick look, she focused her attention on Shera and then stormed into the big office that Shera claimed as her own.

Seconds later, the door shut.

"You don't look happy," Shera said quietly.

"Tear up the contract." She reached into her pocket and pulled out the check. "I don't want this, either. I never wanted it. Do something with it. Donate it to the shelter you sponsor or something."

Slowly, Shera reached out and took the check. "You could use the money, sweetie."

"I don't need the fucking handout. I don't need charity. I don't want the money," Chaili said slowly, enunciating each word. "Either take it, or I'll cash it, come back here with the money and super glue all over that pretty glass table out there in front."

Shera sighed, folded it in half and dropped it on her desk. "I'll make a donation in your name then."

"You can make it in the name of Peter Pan and Captain Hook for all I care. Just don't let me see that damn thing again. And tear up the fucking contract."

Spinning on her heel, she headed to the door.

"Chaili, what's wrong?"

"Nothing. Everything. I'm done with this and if that idiot brother of yours comes by, tell him I'm dead." She glanced over her shoulder as she said it and watched as Shera went pale.

"That's not funny."

Well, damn. Now she was upsetting her friend, who hadn't really done anything. Apparently that foot-in-mouth thing Marc had was contagious. "I'm sorry. Look, just... I can't talk to him, okay?"

She turned to go but Shera caught her arm.

"Marc already called. He wants you to go out tonight. He...ah. Well, he told me not to tell you who was picking you up, either. He seemed really determined." Shera grimaced. "I told him I didn't know if you were free or not and I'd have to get back to him."

"Tell him hell hasn't frozen over, so the answer is no." Curling her hand into a fist, Chaili stared at the back of the door. "I've gotta go."

"What happened?" Shera rested a hand on her arm, leaned in.

That silent, comforting presence was something that just about broke her. Shera was the one who'd been there, all those months. When she'd been so scared...when everybody else just kinda…disappeared.

"I slept with him. Stayed the night." Woodenly, she whispered, "I slept with him, Shera."

"You slept with Marc…"

"Yes."

"Now you're running." Shera winced. "I knew this would happen. Marc has… Ah…"

As Shera opened and closed her mouth, struggling for the words, Chaili started to laugh. It was like the cries of the damned and desperate, painful and sharp. "Oh, Shera. If you're trying to delicately ask if I'm freaked about the fact that Marc has a kinky streak, please don't. I…" She stopped, made herself breathe. Then she had to rub a hand over the ache in her heart as she realized what an ugly bitch this was turning out to be.

A guy who felt like he was her match, in every damn way. And he turned out to be the man she'd loved for…well. Forever. She'd run into a bad marriage just to try and see if she couldn't forget about him, and what a mess *that* had been.

And now this…

Rubbing a finger over her ring, she thought about the things she hadn't shared with Shera. So many parts of her life, she'd shared…but not that. At the time, it had seemed too private. Then, she was too hurt. Then, it just didn't matter.

Sadly, she looked up at Shera. "I'm not freaked. I'm pissed. After the most amazing night of my life, he tells me…'*well, I got my money's worth.*' He called me a whore, Shera. I love him… He gave me the best night of my life. Then he called me a whore."

"You dumb ass."

Marc jumped up at the sound of his sister's voice. He moved so abruptly, he ended up knocking over the piano bench and didn't even care. "You didn't tell her, did you?"

"Tell her what...oh, you mean about the lame-ass plan to take her out tonight?" Her lip curled. "Yes. I told her. She's otherwise engaged."

"Damn it, Shera!"

"Like it would matter." She planted her hands against his chest and shoved him. "You son of a bitch, how could you say that to her?"

"Aw, shit." Turning away from her, he hooked a hand over the back of his neck and stared out over the water. "She told you."

"What in the hell do you expect? She's my best friend. Although, seriously, I was expecting to hear that she was freaked out over your inner-sex-fiend deal, but hell, she really got off on that. But you called her a fucking *whore*?"

Spinning around, he stalked up to her and poked his finger against her shoulder. "I did not. I was nervous as hell, and I said something about getting my money's worth, but I *did* not call her a whore, nor do I think that."

"That's how you made her feel," Shera said quietly. Shaking her head, she reached into her pocket and pulled out a card. "Here. She won't want this. You can keep it. Maybe you'll learn to pull your head out of your ass one of these days."

"I've been trying to do that for thirty-eight years. I speak and dumb shit comes out of my mouth. The only time I can do things right is when I play music or sing," he pointed out, looking down to see the white envelope she was holding out for him. "What's this?"

"It's a thank you note from the lady who took the money at the shelter where I help out a few times a month. Chaili wouldn't take the money for the contract last night and she asked if I'd donate it someplace for her."

Frowning, he stared at the card, his mind rolling back. *Can't afford to lose that account...* Plus, other things. Her working when he'd come over to visit. Even at two or three in the morning, no matter how tired she seemed. "Doesn't she kind of need the money? Isn't that why she's doing the companion thing?"

"She's not *doing* the companion thing," Shera said. She crossed her arms over her chest. "I made her sign the damn contract. She asked why you'd come by and I told her. She said she'd go out with you. She didn't even want to do the contract, take the money, none of it."

A sick feeling settled in his gut. Cold wrapped around his heart. "Why did she want to...?"

"Go out on a date with my big brother?" Shera asked sweetly. She just stared at him. "You used to be halfway smart about women. What in the hell happened? Did all the bad ones screw you up *that* much?"

"Aww. Shit." Crumpling the card in his fist, he hurled it across the room. "I've got to go talk to her."

"Not going to happen today. She's not here. A friend of ours was going up to a cabin she has for a few days. Chaili has an open invite and decided to join her."

"I thought she had a deadline."

"She can work from anywhere, as long as she's got Internet." Shera shrugged. "She said she'd be back in a few days, but I know you...you'll be gone before she gets back so you might as well just give it up."

Like hell.

Chapter Six

Project finished.

It secured her a check that let Chaili pay the typical monthly bills, plus make another dent in the medical hell that was still eating her alive. Looking at the balances on those bills made her head ache. So she didn't look. No reason to, anyway. She knew how much she owed. To the penny. And there were a lot of pennies.

Jumping Jack Pratt, the guy who'd just signed that check, had also given her an invitation to a "little get together" he was having that weekend. He'd winked and mentioned the word *contacts.*

Although the last thing she wanted to do was mingle, it couldn't hurt to make a few contacts with a satisfied customer. And hey, if she was out there, trying to act all professional, then she wasn't stuck in her apartment with a suitcase she still hadn't unpacked, stuck there, thinking about last weekend, stuck there where she just might start to cry if she looked at any one spot too long, because damn it, she had little signs of him everywhere.

Every damned CD.

Pictures of her with him and Shera.

She needed to do something about this, she realized... Of course, she needed to go to the party, but—

"No. Now, before I change my mind," she whispered. Grabbing a plastic crate, she dumped the CDs into it, pictures, everything that had anything to do with Marc. She had to cut this out of her, out of her heart, out of her soul, out of her life. It was going to be kind of like lancing a wound. It would hurt like hell, but she was already hurting. Once she did it and suffered through the initial pain, it would get better.

She kept pieces of Marc around her because it made it easier to pretend. She lost herself in fantasies, or just let herself think about him more than she should. Even though she knew it was foolishness.

There wasn't ever going to be a *them*. Ever. And she'd known that. Really. She'd never expected them to have a night, much less anything more. She'd screwed up by trying to grab for a chance to have a *real* memory of just them. Only them. Like a pretend *them*. If she hadn't done that, she could have happily existed forever in her little make-believe world, but she'd done it and now she had to deal with the consequences.

The crate was overflowing as she pushed into Shera's house. She dealt with the alarm and grabbed a piece of paper, jotted a note.

I'm clearing this stuff out. If you want the pictures, take them. I figured you could give the CDs and shit to the shelter. They probably need the music. Although maybe they can auction off the signed ones...I don't know. Whatever you want to do with it. Was invited to a party @ J. Pratt's house. Supposed to mingle, maybe make some more contacts for work. Later.

Without letting herself look back at the bits and pieces of a dead dream, she reset the alarm and left. She needed to change. Figure out what she had in her wardrobe that would work for a summer "get together" for a rich, arrogant, son-of-a-bitch.

Staring at the note, Marc called his sister. As soon as she came on the line, he demanded, "Who in the hell is J. Pratt?"

"Ah...Marc?"

"No. It's the Easter Bunny. I heard you were good and I wanted to leave a present at your house. Hope you don't mind I'm a few months late," he said, staring at the crate in front of him. Normally, it made him feel damned weird to see shit like this in the house of somebody he knew.

But this wasn't just his career.

He saw a stub from a show they'd all gone to see in high school. Springsteen. They'd snuck out, even though their folks would have killed them. Well, Marc and Shera's mom would have. Chaili's mom...she might have cared if she could have pulled herself out of a bottle.

A poster from his first tour.

A couple of T-shirts with the band's logo on them.

There was a strip of pictures, the kind where you had to wedge yourself into a photo booth. He remembered that. They'd taken it up on the pier, right before everything took off.

She'd kept all of this.

"J. Pratt, sis," he said as he lifted the crate.

"Hell, I don't know. Probably Prattle Enterprises. That disc jockey guy who decided he'd start his own radio show after the station laid him off...? I *think*. And why are you asking?"

J. Pratt.

Disconnecting the phone, he headed to the front door. He only barely remembered to reset the alarm on his way out and he had to juggle to do it.

Yep. J. Pratt was a disc jockey. A search on his phone showed him that.

And down at the bottom of his website, he saw the discreet little line indicating who'd designed the guy's site.

Glory Daze Designs.

He put the crate into his trunk, although that strip of pictures he slid into his shirt pocket. Once he was in the car, he called his assistant. "I need an address...a local disc jockey. J. Pratt."

Ilona was quiet for a minute and then asked, "J. Pratt. As in Jumping Jack Pratt? Big radio hotshot?"

"Hell if I know. All I know is the guy is a disc jockey and I think he's having a party today. I need to know where he lives."

"He lives about a mile away from us. And yes, he's a disc jockey. He's also one of the biggest assholes known to man and yes...he's having a party. I know this because he's made sure to call the house about three times this week to invite Miguel."

Miguel... Marc ran his tongue along his teeth. "So...what's my favorite drummer up to?"

"Don't, Marc. He'll kick your ass if you even ask him. We can't stand that guy." Ilona snorted, her voice thick with disgust. "He can't look at a woman without checking out her tits. He can't talk to a woman without checking out her tits. The only reason he even invites us over there to check out my rack and grill us about you, anyway."

"What do I have to do with your rack? I never even noticed you have one."

"Gee, thanks." Ilona sighed.

In the background, Marc heard Miguel's voice. "Are you talking to Marc about your rack?"

"Now you're going to get me in trouble," Marc muttered.

"Relax. You're more interested in my brains than my boobs. That's a good thing. Hold on. If you're serious, you can talk to your favorite drummer. But leave me out of it. Completely."

Marc drummed his fingers on the steering wheel, staring off down the street. A car rolled by and he automatically turned his head, staring toward Shera's house.

"What's this about your favorite drummer? I'm the only drummer who's ever been dumb enough to work with your dumb ass," Miguel said, his voice amused. "And why were you talking about my girl's boobs?"

"She was talking about them. Not me. I heard you were invited to a party."

Miguel's sneer was evident in his voice. "Jumping Jackhole's thing? Not my idea of a party. All he does is kiss ass and wheedle."

"We deal with that on a daily basis."

"Not when we're on break." Miguel muttered under his breath and finally asked, "What's up, buddy?"

"I need to go to that party."

"And you want me to take you. You got any idea how annoying that fucker is?"

Another car drove by and this one slowed down, took a longer look. Marc could feel the guy's gaze resting on him, despite the fact that Marc had his head turned, a pair of sunglasses on and a hat. Shit. Time to go. Starting the car, he tossed the phone down and switched it to speaker. He hated headsets. "I don't care about the DJ. There's a..." He blew out a breath and tried to figure out what to say. His closest friends had developed this insane protective streak over him and although part of him understood, he wasn't some idiot kid.

Okay, so he did idiot stuff, but that was his own problem.

And this wasn't idiot stuff.

This was Chaili.

He'd been waiting a week to finally talk to her and he knew she was home, because the sweet Mrs. Hornby across the way had promised to call as soon as she saw Chaili's car. Because of course, Marc's sister wasn't telling him a damn thing. But Mrs. Hornby had. It was just Marc's dumb luck he'd been down in his gym, without his phone, when she'd called, and by the time he'd emerged an hour later and then showered and made the drive to her place...Chaili was gone.

But he also knew sometimes Chaili left notes for Shera in the house, an old habit. And hot damn, he'd found the note, along with the bits and pieces of their life together...bits and pieces she was throwing away.

It made him hurt to see it and he couldn't even explain why. Had he fucked up that bad?

He'd spent the whole damn week rehearsing what he'd say to her, but then he'd seen the evidence that maybe it wouldn't matter... No. He wasn't going to think that way. It would matter. It had to, because he was thinking maybe the reason he always felt that vague emptiness inside him, why no woman seemed to click with him, was because she wasn't the right one.

Chaili had always felt right.

Always.

And he wasn't going to let her cut him out just because he was an absolute fuckhead from time to time.

"There's a woman there. Don't go freaking out—this isn't Selene, it's not Lily or anybody else like them. I've known her most of my life and this...shit." Did he tell him it was Chaili? Miguel knew her...and Marc didn't know if that would make things better or worse. Okay. So he didn't tell his friend. Yet. He'd figure it out soon. "It doesn't matter. She's going to be there, I think, and I need to see her."

For a long moment, Miguel said nothing. Then finally, he sighed and said, "Okay, man. Pick me up. But don't be surprised when that bloodsucking tick attaches himself to your ass."

Chapter Seven

Jumping Jack Pratt was one of her biggest accounts.

Next to the website she designed and maintained for *Escortè*, this was her *biggest* account and Chaili kept that in mind as she felt his gaze crawling over her. *Waste of time, pal.*

The top she wore had a draped neck, fitting her lean torso and camouflaging the fact that she'd never be filling out a bikini the right way again. Well, she'd never really filled one out very well to begin with, but now?

That didn't keep Jumping Jack from trying to sneak a peek. He angled in a little closer under the pretense of whispering in her ear. "Would you like me to introduce you around?"

"I've got it, thanks," she said easily. "I don't want to look like I'm trying to hog the host's attention."

He didn't get the point. Most of the women there were ignoring him. Apparently, he'd worn out his welcome at their elbow. Suppressing a sigh, she headed over to the punch bowl and refilled her glass, wondered how much longer she should bother trying to stay. She wasn't making contacts here. She wasn't doing anything but getting annoyed and—

"Son of a bitch, he came," Jack muttered. He went rigid next to her and he gripped her arm, squeezing excitedly. "And...oh. Shit. I think I just creamed my pants. Babe, I gotta go. Have fun, okay." He swatted her on the ass and while she stood there, her jaw hanging open, he lost himself in the crowd.

"That's probably the most action you've seen in years," a

low, familiar voice said.

The sound of it was enough to make her skin crawl.

Slowly, she looked up and found herself staring into a pair of eyes that had once made her feel...well, mostly happy. She'd never been ready to dance around on a mountain side when she'd been married to Tim, but she'd been happy enough. She'd thought they suited each other.

And then her life came apart at the seams.

She touched the ring she wore—a ring Shera had given her the day her divorce was final. As she stood there staring at her ex-husband, Chaili remembered what Shera had told her the day her divorce was final. The ring—a twisted band of oxidized silver—was designed around the ruby that had once been part of her wedding set. *It's a reminder of you...it's remade. Like you. Only better...silver is stronger than gold, right?*

Chaili had worn it every day for the past three years. Remade. Stronger than gold. And maybe a little tarnished.

With a cool smile, she met Tim's bland gray eyes. "Action...I barely even know what it is," she drawled. "You did a lousy job teaching me, after all."

A faint smiled curled his lips and he tipped his glass. "I kind of miss those claws of yours." Then he glanced over and lifted a hand.

A woman came over, placed her hand in Tim's and stood there, silently, head bowed. All nice, demure and submissive. The way Tim had wanted her to be.

It wouldn't have ever happened. Things had started getting dicey between them even before Chaili's...problem. All because she wouldn't be his little submissive in all things.

Oh fucking well. Looked like he'd found one. Judging from the look in his eyes, he was waiting for a reaction too. But if he thought the sight of the big-breasted, blonde doll-baby was going to bother her, he needed to get his head examined.

Maybe they were happy together. Not that she cared about Tim being happy, but Tim's asshole tendencies weren't this kid's fault. Holding a hand, she said, "Hi. I'm Chaili. Tim and I were once married. It's one of the less pleasant facts of my past."

"Ouch," Tim joked, resting a hand on his chest. "But there are so many pleasant things we shared before..."

His gaze dropped.

Chaili lifted her glass to her lips, studied him over the rim for a long moment. "You need to watch it, man. You'd hate for me to make a scene, after all."

"Now, you won't do that." He winked at her. "You never were much for public displays, right?"

"You'd be amazed at how things have changed."

"Chaili."

The low rasp of *that* voice made her shiver. Oh, now this was just wrong, she thought wearily. Wrong on so many levels. Although she understood now why in the hell Jumping Jack had been yapping about creaming his pants. And eeewww, what an image. Chaili tossed back the rest of the punch, put the glass down and turned to stare into golden eyes.

"Marc."

He flicked a look past her shoulder and then looked back at her. "Maybe we can have that talk now," he said.

"What talk?" She gave him a brilliant smile.

"The one you've been avoiding for a week." Holding out a hand, Marc stood there. Waiting.

"Um, is that...?"

"Be quiet, Nina," Tim said, his voice sour. "Marc. How nice

to see you again."

A scowl darkened Marc's face and he took another, longer look at Tim. She saw the moment he recognized her ex. The two men hadn't ever spent much time around each other and she had the impression Marc hadn't liked her choice in husbands. Looking back, she realized sometimes he showed moments of true wisdom.

"Tim," he bit off, his voice curt. Then he looked back at her and the hard glint in his eyes softened. "Chaili, please."

Her heart just wanted to shatter. Or maybe it wanted to melt. She didn't know. But then she reminded herself. She was done with this. With dreaming about him and—

"Hell, Marc. Why you wasting time on a bitch like her?" Tim said, his voice thick and scathing. "Dude like you, you ought to be dating one of those Kardashian babes or some starlet or something. Chaili's damaged goods, you know."

Shame hit her hard. Fast. But even as it came on, she shoved it down. Anger bit into her. *Damaged?* Staring at her ex-husband, she could have kicked herself for even letting herself *feel* ashamed. *Damaged?*

She didn't even realize she was moving until she'd already snatched the glass from Marc's hand and tossed the contents into Tim's face.

His face went red. She curled her lip at him and saw him moving, braced herself to block the punch she saw coming, but she was pushed out of the way and two seconds later, Tim was on the ground, one big, angry man crouched over him.

Damaged goods—

Blood roared in his ears and he didn't know what had him more enraged. The fact that this son of a mother-fucking *bitch* had been that close to hitting Chaili, or what he'd just said about her.

"I ever see you lift a hand to her," he whispered, bending down until he was speaking directly into Tim's ear. "I'm going to gut you. And I'll do it slow, my man. You hear me?"

Tim panted, his face still red, eyes snapping with fury. "Hell, she *likes* it when a man raises his hand to her, don't you know that?" He tried to smile, but it fell apart. "Come on, buddy. I've seen where you go. I've been to Blue's too. I know what you like...haven't you figured out what she's into yet? She likes it."

"Oh, now that was the completely wrong thing to say," Marc purred, his hand curling into a fist, muscles bunching. He could see the color red—splashing in his mind as he plowed a fist into Tim's face. Red, one of the colors he saw pretty well, and just then he wanted to see it damn bad, spreading out in a fountain over Tim's face. "I'm not going to wait to hurt you. I'm just going to do it now."

"Stop it, Marc."

It was probably the only voice that could have gotten through to him.

Slowly, he dragged his eyes away from the man he really wanted to beat bloody and stared into Chaili's face. She was crouched by Tim's head, her elbows resting on her knees. As he stared at her, she shook her head. "Don't. If you do, it's just going to cause you more trouble and you get enough of that on your own. You don't need to pick up *my* trouble."

Her vivid eyes rested on his, steadily. And she wasn't trying to get away from him.

Okay.

Blinking, he blew out a breath and looked back into Tim's face. Damn it, he wanted to see him bleed.

"You don't want me to hit him," he said slowly.

"No."

"Shit." Letting go of Tim's shirt, he remained crouched over him for a minute. "You want to watch what you say, what you do. Shut the hell up, don't look at her...don't speak to her. Don't speak *about* her." Then he made himself look away from Tim before he did what he so badly wanted to do. As he straightened, he kept his eyes focused on Chaili, staring at her, only at her. "Leave with me. Talk to me."

"Ahh..." She backed away a step.

He narrowed his eyes and glanced down at Tim who was scrambling his way to his feet. "Well, I can always finish what I started, I guess."

Chaili rolled her eyes. "Now that's just juvenile."

"Fine. I'm juvenile. It will feel damn good."

"Damn it, people are watching," Chaili hissed, stepping in closer.

"Like I give a flying fuck." He tossed her a reckless grin.

"You stupid son of a bitch." She continued to glare at him.

But as he took a step away, she caught his hand. "Fine." She glanced around and gave her ex-husband a mock look of concern. "Damn it, Tim, you should be more careful. You didn't hurt anything when you slipped, did you?"

"You crazy bitch, I—"

Nina—that was her name, Marc thought, leaned in, caught Tim's arm, giving him a wide-eyed look, shaking her head.

"Tim, dude, you always were a clumsy freak," Miguel said from behind. "You shouldn't go hitting the punch so hard. It's got a kick to it, ya know."

Hell, Marc had forgotten about him.

Shooting his friend a look, Marc tried to figure out what to do about getting *him* home when he had to get Chaili out of here before she changed her mind.

"I'm going to go call my lady," Miguel said, sighing. "I think I ate too much." He patted his belly and turned away, heading into the crowd.

As people started to press in closer, Marc pushed his way through, gripping Chaili's hand. "Let's go."

"Go?" Jumping Jack demanded. "But you just got here?"

"And I got who I came for," Marc said, still holding on to her hand, praying she wouldn't slip away. He could make this right, damn it. He could do it. Of course, it would be easier if he could do it without talking.

Chapter Eight

"Your ex is a bigger asshole than I remember," Marc said after thirty minutes of silence.

"Yes." She stared out the window, her gaze focused on the lake. "Where are we going?"

He drummed a hand on the steering wheel. "I don't know. Where do you want to go?"

Sighing, she rested her head on the back of the seat. "Home. I'm tired."

"If I take you home, are you going to talk to me?"

"I'm talking now, aren't I?"

From the corner of her eye, she saw him gripping the staring wheel so tight his hands were almost bloodless. "You're not talking to me," he said quietly. "You're talking through me. Looking through me. Around me. I was an asshole and I'm sorry and I'm trying to make it right and you won't let me and it's killing me."

She was pretty certain her heart cracked. Right down the middle. Damn it. She was ready to be *done* with him. She *wanted* to be done with him. But how could she do that when he kept pushing himself inside her like that? And why *now?* When she was determined to excise him?

Part of her, the angry part of her that had waited and yearned for so long before giving up hope, wanted to tell him to fuck off. Another part of her still hoped. But the part of her that took control was the part that just couldn't stand to see him hurting. She'd loved him for too long. And hell, he was a friend.

They had to find a way to make this right. Get things level, and then they could move past it.

"We can talk, Marc," she said, rubbing her thumb over the bumpy surface of her ring. *Remade,* she told herself. She could remake herself again, remake the shattered pieces of her heart, but not until she handled this part first.

Damaged goods.

It bumped around in his head, didn't want to settle.

What the fuck...

No. Not now. Not now, he told himself as he followed her up the stairs and into to her apartment. Dipping a hand into his pocket, he rubbed his thumb over the ticket stub to the Springsteen concert, felt the worn, smooth surface. He had both the stub and one picture from the pier with him, holding them like good luck charms.

He needed to do this and get it done first, see if he could get her to believe him, get her to accept him and give him another chance.

That was what he needed to focus on.

And yet, as Chaili turned around to face him, without him even realizing what he was going to say, he blurted out, "You were raped, weren't you?"

She blinked, looked a little thrown off. Then she sighed, passed a hand over her face. "No, Marc. I wasn't raped."

"If you were, you can tell me. I mean...I want to kill whoever..." And he would, damn it. He'd find him. Kill him slow and...

"I wasn't raped." She turned away and moved to the

window, staring outside. "Damn that son of a bitch."

"What...hell. You know what? Doesn't matter." He stared at the back of her head, willing her to turn, to look at him. "He's a dumb prick, running his mouth off..."

Chaili reached for the hem of her shirt and dragged it off.

Then she turned around.

The first thing that caught his gaze was the tattoo. It was pretty, he noticed inanely. And there was no mistaking the pink ribbon, and the ribbon made up the body of what looked to be a butterfly, the wings spreading out to cover the altered planes of her chest. The wings were vividly blue-green against her skin, the pink ribbon an elegant, graceful swirl.

The scars were surgically neat on her seemingly frail torso. One of them was all but hidden in the wings of the tattoo, but he could still see it.

Her skin looked so fragile, stretched tightly over her ribcage, the flat expanse marred only by the scars...and that elegant, graceful tattoo that told the story so very plainly.

Below it were the words:

Hope. Courage. Will.

Stunned, he stared, the blood roaring in his ears, his heart wrenching in his chest.

Cancer...you had cancer and you never told me.

Tearing his gaze from her chest, he stared into her eyes. Swallowing, he rasped out, "When?"

"I had the mastectomy just over three years ago. Right before the divorce was final, incidentally." She threw the shirt down and sauntered over to the chair, flinging her long, lean body down in it, and stared at him, her chin propped on her fist. "As you can see, Marc, I'm pretty damn damaged."

"The hell you are," he growled, stalking over to her. He

should have pounded Tim into a bloody, bruised pulp. Going to his knees next to her chair, he went to say something, but found himself staring at the scars again. At the tattoo. At the marks of the pain, the fear she must have suffered...alone. At the mark she'd given herself. How she'd survived. Risen above it. "He divorced you over this."

"Oh, he didn't divorce me because of the mastectomy," she said, her voice lazy. But the glint in her eyes was weird, a hard, almost manic little light. "He divorced me because he didn't really love me. I didn't really love him, either, so that's fair. Things had been rough between us for a while. Still, it might have been nice if he'd stuck it out with me until I was through the treatments, the surgery. But he didn't want to deal with me being sick. Maybe losing my hair—that really worried him. And I did. Man, he would have loathed that. But what really bothered him was the freak I'd be when the surgery was done... I lost everything, as you can see. It was pretty advanced and the only way to save me was to take it all. He didn't want to live with a deformed freak."

Snaking his hand out, he clamped it around the back of her neck and tugged her in, slanting his mouth over hers. "Stop," he rasped against her lips. "You're not a freak. You're not..."

And to his disgust, he felt something burning his eyes.

Shoving upright, he started to pace. "How in the hell didn't I know about this?" he demanded, turning to glare at her. "Shit, Chaili, you're one of the few people I actually consider a *real* friend and I don't hear about something like this? What the hell?"

"Maybe you would have...if you were ever here." She shrugged and crossed one leg over the other. "But you weren't. After you left for the '09 tour, it was eleven months before you came back home and by then, the surgery was done. What do you think I should have done? Whip up my shirt on one of the rare times you came by to see your sister?"

"I..." Groaning, he covered his face with his hands. Yeah. He'd stayed away for a long time because it was easier. He'd fucked up so often, and it was so much easier just to hide from his life. He'd fucked up with Lily. And there was the fiasco from a few years earlier with another girlfriend he hadn't ever told anybody about, not even his sister. His lawyer knew, but that was it.

Shera had warned him about Lily. She'd tried her hardest, he had to give her that.

He hadn't listened.

He'd gotten himself screwed over.

And the worst part was he knew he deserved it.

Why should he come home and try to have any kind of life when all he did was screw it up?

Still...

He hadn't come home and he'd spent years missing one of his closest friends and because of it, he'd ended up missing something that he damned well should have known about. Cancer, for fuck's sake. She had cancer.

And she'd been alone.

He stopped by the back window, staring out over the backyard. "You were alone through the whole damn thing, weren't you?"

The rigid line of his shoulders, the way his voice was gruffer than normal had her heart shuddering a little. She couldn't block out how his voice affected her, but if she didn't look at him, maybe, just maybe she could get through this. Looking away, she said, "No. I wasn't alone. Shera was there. She hired extra help at the office so she could be around." Glancing over the apartment, she added, "She offered me the apartment here. I...well, I was looking for a place but..." The pride she'd had to swallow so often over the past few years crept up. She wasn't going into that with him. No way. No how. "It was just easier, being around somebody. She tried to give me some lame excuse that it would save her from having deadbeats trying to rent the place, but I think we both needed each other then. I never meant for it to be long term but here I am."

Broke. Busting her ass to pay the medical bills. But mostly at peace with things, she guessed.

Or she had been. And then she'd made that fatal mistake a week ago. Reaching for something she was never meant to have, even if it was just for a little while.

A hand closed over her knee. Startled, she swung her gaze around and realized Marc had come back to her. Golden eyes, burning with intensity, stared into hers. "I hate that I didn't know. I hate that you didn't have somebody with you."

"I did. Shera—"

"It's not the same." His lip curled, a disgusted look on his face. "That son of a bitch walked when you needed him most. I never liked that bastard...you deserved so much better, but I never thought he was that low, to leave you when you'd need somebody the most."

She watched as his gaze dipped back to her chest and she fought the urge to pull her shirt back on. She'd come to grips with how she looked. She wasn't going to cringe away from her appearance. Still, this was worse than being stripped bare. Worse than being naked. She couldn't handle seeing pity in his eyes and she couldn't handle it if she saw repulsion either.

Falling back on the mocking humor that had been her

shield for so long, she smirked at him. "It's a pretty sight, isn't it? Not hard to understand why he didn't want to hang around when this was going to be the end result."

"Stop it."

"I mean, I was never exactly stacked. I barely even filled out an A cup, but these days—*hey, damn it!*" She went from sprawling on the couch to half sprawled against his chest. His hand cupped the back of her neck and the gold in his eyes all but sparked with anger. "Damn it, what in the hell is your problem?"

Instead of answering that question, Marc banded an arm around her waist, locking her against him before he asked a question of his own. "Tell me something...how did you get hooked up with that stupid fuck? He doesn't deserve you. Didn't then, doesn't now. How did the two of you happen?"

Chaili tried for one second to twist away from him before going still, glaring at him. "What?"

"I want to know. How did the two of you get together? Why did you marry him? You already told me you didn't love him. So why marry him?"

"We met through a couple of friends," she snapped. "He asked me out, I said yes. We were compatible. After a few months, he asked me to marry him and I said yes. No, I didn't love him and, no, he didn't love me and we never pretended otherwise. But we clicked in other areas and that worked for us."

His eyes narrowed. "You settled for compatible. Shit, Chaili. What in the hell does that mean, anyway?"

"It means I wasn't going to get what I really wanted, so I might as well be with somebody who could make me happy enough. It wasn't perfect but so what?" She couldn't look at him while she talked about this. If she did, he was going to see what it was she *did* want. *Who* she wanted. All but dying inside for want of him, it seemed.

His hand traced up her back and she shivered, her lashes drifting shut. One finger stroked over one of the scars along her side. All the scars were neat, faded now, but they were still scars. Still harsh reminders. She didn't even look like a boy. Skin stretched tight over her ribs. A few of the women she knew through the support groups had gotten breast reconstruction, but it wasn't an option for her and she doubted she'd bother with it even if she could afford it.

"You should go after who you want, not what's available," he whispered, pressing his lips against her shoulder.

Yeah. She'd tried that. Had ended with her heart shattered in her hands this last time around. And the first time she'd tried to go after Marc, he'd all but patted her on the head.

Of course, *now* those strong hands were stroking over her body, one palm curving over her ass. The other hand fisted in her hair and dragged her head back. "Just how were you compatible, Chaili?" he whispered, staring into her eyes.

She felt the dull rush of blood creeping up her cheeks as he watched her. Chaili wasn't ashamed of what she liked. Not now. She had been, for a while. But after the hell she'd gone through with the diagnosis, the surgery, the treatment, all the while dealing with a divorce...she knew who she was.

But it was unsettling, to say the least, to discuss something like this.

"Oh, come on," she said, shooting for a smart-ass smile. "You heard him. I've got a thing for being hit. You probably noticed I get off on being bossed around too. He has a thing for spanking and giving orders. We were a decent match."

As he lifted a hand, traced it down her shoulder, down her arm until he could catch her wrist, he said gruffly, "A thing for

107

being hit. Chaili...there's a difference between what you want and being hit." He braceleted her wrist, drew it behind her back. Repeated it on the other side. Securing both of her wrists in one hand, he used his hold on her to tug her back, bowing her spine as he bent forward and pressed his lips to the center of the tattoo, where the wings flared out from the ribbon. "If he thinks 'being hit' is giving you what you need, then he's a clueless dick. You settled, baby girl, and you settled awful damn low."

Her breath hitched in her throat as she stared at his bent head. His lips feathered over the delicate lines and swirls of the tattoo, the flare of the wings. Heat flooded her, rising from her chest, spreading up over her neck to suffuse her face.

I shouldn't do this, shouldn't be sitting here with him... Blood pulsed inside her veins, a hot, teasing sensation that was far more erotic that she could recall experiencing before.

When he shifted his attention to the scars, though, she tried to twist away.

His free arm caught her, pinned her in place.

"Just how did he make you feel? Did he make you happy?" he whispered before he used his tongue to trace the line of one neat, pale scar.

"We gave each other what we needed," she said, trying for casual but failing. Her voice skipped, caught.

"No. You scratched an itch," Marc said, moving to the other scar. "I'll give you what you need. What you want... Things you probably don't let yourself think about."

"Hmmm. Arrogant, much?" She blinked her eyes. Damn it, she wasn't suddenly seeing him through a veil of tears. That wasn't happening. And he *wasn't* right. She'd been okay with Tim. She'd been happy. For a while, at least.

Swallowing around the knot swelling in her throat, she

jeered at him as he reached up and stroked his thumb along one of her scars, tracing to where it ran under her arm before it ended. "What's up, Marc? You want a freaky fuck for your memory book?"

"It's not going to work, Chaili. You're trying to push me away. I'm not going anywhere." From under his lashes, he continued to stroke the scar, as though he was learning it by touch. "This doesn't faze me. Doesn't bother me."

"That's why you can't stop staring," she said sourly. "Why you can't seem to stop petting the damn things. You got a scar fetish?"

"I can't stop staring at you. Don't want to stop touching. And I just might have a fetish, but it's not about the damn scars." He used his hold on her wrists to bring her closer, sinking his teeth into her lower lip until she gasped.

Then she shuddered as he licked the small hurt and sucked it into his mouth. "You're expecting me to stare," he said, his voice flat and unyielding. "That's why you did this... You wanted me to stare, wanted to shock the hell out of me and make me freak and run."

Abruptly, he let go of her wrists and caught her head between his hands, slanted his mouth over hers. Against her lips, he rasped, "I'm not running...got that?"

When he kissed her, she opened for him, unable to do anything else.

When he stood, supporting her weight with his own, she wrapped her legs around his waist and clung to him.

And when he lifted his head, long moments later, she tried to pull him back to her. If he would just never, ever stop kissing her, maybe she wouldn't have to think. Maybe she wouldn't have to worry and maybe she wouldn't have to think about how damned scared she was. About how screwed up she still was...after all this time.

She'd thought she'd dealt with what Tim had done, but damn it, she hadn't.

Large hands stroked down her back, cupped her ass, squeezing through the denim. "You're not going to hide this time, Chaili," he said quietly. "Not again. Not ever."

There were tears in her eyes, and it hurt his heart to see them. Tears that made her eyes gleam even as she tried to hide them, dipping her head so he wouldn't see. But he wasn't letting her hide anything.

Cupping her chin in his hand, he kissed one eye, then the other, before reaching behind him and unhooking her ankles. "No more hiding," he murmured against her lips.

"And what about you?" she whispered, her hands resting on his waist, kneading the flesh just above his hips restlessly. "You've been hiding a hell of a lot too."

"No hiding. Not either of us." He just hoped he didn't fuck it up all to hell. "Go to your room. Get naked. But I don't want you getting under covers."

Her lashes dipped. "Be careful how far you push me, Marc. I can only do so much," she warned him quietly.

He had a feeling she could handle more than she realized, but they'd figure out boundaries and shit later. The only thing he wanted her to do was stop hiding from him. Shy. She was about as shy as he was. She'd just wanted to keep him from seeing the scars. Part of him could understand why, but she'd shown him and there was no point in trying to close that door now.

After she'd disappeared around the corner that led to her bedroom, he reached into his pocket and pulled out the picture, the ticket stub. There had been only one of the two of them. The others had all had Shera, Chaili and him. This one, though, it was just Chaili and him. She'd been laughing at him while he was making a face at her.

There had been a light in her eyes. One he realized he hadn't seen in a good long while.

Whether it had been the cancer that had taken the light away, or just how fucking hard life had been since then, he didn't know.

But he was going to put that light back in her eyes.

Slipping out of his jacket, he tossed it on the back of the couch, tucked the picture in the pocket. He kicked out of his shoes and socks and left them there as well. He left his shirt and jeans on, and on the way out of the room, he paused by a coat rack. Draped over one of the pegs was a knit scarf, it looked blue to him so it was likely some shade of green and he could see threads of silver twisting through it.

He took it down, rubbing the nubby weave between his fingers, twining it round and round his wrist.

It had been almost two minutes.

He killed another minute by stopping in her bathroom. It was neat as a pin, ruthlessly organized and showing no sign of anybody's presence but hers.

He checked the miniscule closet, the cabinet under the sink, all without finding what he needed.

She'd closed the door to her bedroom most of the way. Pushing it open, he paused, his breath lodging in his throat as he saw her sitting on the edge of the bed, her legs crossed, hands folded neatly in her lap and a glint in her eyes as she stared at him.

The lights were off. Thick curtains, nearly the same shade

as the scarf, blocked out the light. He hit the lights and watched as a minute flinch tightened her body before she relaxed. Chaili lowered her head and her shoulders rose and fell on a deep breath.

Without saying another word, he ambled over to the bed and dropped the scarf next to her, watching her tremble as she glanced at it. Turning away, he circled the room, eyeing the neat little desk, sans computer, sitting by the window.

He studied the neat stack of books, some with stickers from a used bookstore, others with the little tag that indicated they were from a library. Romance, urban fantasy... She'd always loved to read. And she'd hoarded her books too. There was also a huge, whopping stack of bills. He continued his trek around the room until he came to the nightstand by her bed. Crouching down next to it, he pulled open a drawer...bingo.

There were a couple vibrators there. Lubricant. He pulled out one of the vibrators—it was one that had an extra extension for the anus. As he turned it on, he glanced back at Chaili. Her face was flushed but she continued to stare at him, that glint still in her eyes.

"You like anal?"

"No. I just figured I'd shell out some cash for a vibrator like that for no reason," she said, giving him a snotty little smile before lifting a hand and studying her nails.

"Smart ass."

"Hmmm."

He turned it off and tossed it on the bed, along with the lubricant and then a silver bullet that he saw tucked in the corner.

"You have a pair of scissors handy?"

She glanced at the desk behind him. "Over there."

He found them, tucked in a neat little cup with a pens and pencils. He put the scissors on the bedside table but she didn't even glance at them, nor did she seem all that concerned about the scarf he held. He wrapped it around his hands, watched as her gaze flicked down to it, lingered and then she went back to studying her nails.

"Stand up," he told her.

She just sat there.

"Stand up," he growled.

Lowering her hand, she lifted her head and stared at him for a long second before slowly rising to her feet.

"I want a couple of things clear," he said quietly. "First...I think you're beautiful. You've always been beautiful, and nothing changes that." Laying his palm against her chest so that it covered one of the scars, he said, "This sure as hell doesn't. Got it?"

Her only response was to blink, but he saw something glinting wet, diamond bright in her eyes.

"Second...I'm going to say shitty things, and do shitty things. You know that...are you going to hold it against me?"

Chaili curled her lip. "That depends...are you going to make the implication that I'm a whore again?"

"No." A sick feeling twisted in his gut. "And I'm damned sorry I made you feel that way, because I know you're not, and I don't think of you that way. Are we clear on that?"

"We're clear."

"I won't ever hurt you in a way you don't like during sex, although we need to figure out the stopping limits. I'm talking about everything else. Like what happened last week. I'm damned good at putting my foot in my mouth and I'm damned good at screwing up. Are you going to ignore me every time I'm an asshole?"

He continued to keep his hand over her chest, stroking his thumb over the frail skin.

"If I did that, I'd never speak to you—never would have spoken to you after I met you when I was about twelve," she said, sniffing a little. "Next to playing the piano and singing, being an asshole is one of your finer talents in life."

With a wry grin, he muttered, "You know me well."

Studying her face, he said, "We need to talk more later, but this isn't a one-time, or a two-time thing. If that's a problem, tell me now."

Chaili just continued to watch him.

He hoped she couldn't hear the excited little dance his heart was doing.

"About those limits, we'll talk about them more later. Although I kind of hate some of the stupid shit some people use with this stuff...I think it's a good idea to set guidelines and ground rules. For now, I just want a word you can use if I'm going too far or hurting you."

"I take it asshole isn't a good one."

He jerked her against him and palmed her ass. "Probably not. I have plans on fucking yours here shortly so that's probably not ideal."

Her eyes widened and her pupils spiked, flared. As a rosy flush settled on her cheeks, she touched her tongue to her lips. "Ah...taco," she blurted out.

"Taco?" he asked, amused, tracing the line between the cheeks of her ass, watching her lashes drift down, listening to the way her breathing hitched.

"Yes."

"Gotcha. Taco, it is." He let her go and said, "Turn around

and put your hands on the bed."

Chaili took her time doing so, but it wasn't so much to push his buttons and see just how far he was going to go. It was because she couldn't get her damn legs to work.

This was really happening. Her knees felt like butter and her heart was slamming against her ribs so hard she couldn't breathe. She'd almost come to grips with the fact that she'd had some seriously hot sex with Marc, but he was a guy, right? Guys were into sex and she'd been available, but this...

He stroked a hand down her spine, cupped her ass.

This was more than sex.

He'd seen her—her scarred, imperfect body—and he still wanted her.

He lifted his hand and brought it down on her ass. Hard. The pleasure of it jolted through her side by side with the pain and she cried out, her fingers curling into the nubby fabric of her comforter, seeking out something to ground herself with.

He paused, waiting. She squeezed her eyes closed, desperate, ready for him to do it again. The only time Tim had ever done this—

No. Don't think about him...

Marc spanked her again. She moaned as the delicious sensation rolled through her, spreading upward, outward.

Again. Again. On the fifth one, her knees buckled and if he hadn't caught her with his hands around her hips, she would have ended up on the floor.

He kept a hand on her hips, steadying her as he traced over the sensitive flesh of her butt, the skin still stinging from his attention. "I like seeing your skin turn pink," he said, his voice still level but just a little more hoarse than normal. A little more edgy and raw.

His voice was just another sensation, stroking over her like silk, rubbing against sensitive nerve endings, making her burn so very badly. "Get on the bed," he rasped.

She eased away and went to get on her hands and knees, but he stopped her. "On your back. I want to see you spread out under me."

Closing her eyes, she hunched her shoulders. Behind her, he waited, one hand on her hip. "No more hiding."

No hiding. She pulled away and turned, sat on the edge and scooted back. The busted box springs of the broken-down mattress made an awful sound but she ignored it, staring instead at his hands as he reached for the bottom of his shirt to drag it off.

Man, she loved his hands...

He put one knee on the edge of the bed. "Lie back for me."

Okay. She could do this...

He was looking at her face, anyway, right?

But then he reached for the vibrator. Oh, hell.

Her breathing caught and she watched as a wicked little grin canted up the corner of his beautiful mouth. She just wanted to eat him sometimes, hold his face in her hands and kiss him until they were stupid with it and then work on down...

"What are you thinking?" he asked softly.

Catching her lip between her teeth, she studied him. Man, if he had been one of the few lovers she'd had before hooking up with Tim, she could have told him. Easily. Tim had never been one for wanting to know her thoughts, but the others...yeah. They'd been pretty good. Tim...well, he'd pushed all her kink buttons, but he'd never wanted to *talk* with her.

If she hadn't been reeling emotionally and just looking for something, she never would have married him, she knew.

But it was harder to tell Marc.

Because Marc was the only man who'd ever managed to really *matter*.

"I'm thinking I'd like to kiss you stupid," she finally said. "Then I'd liked to get on my knees and take you in my mouth and see if I could make you feel about as weak and crazy as you make me."

Something flared in his eyes, a wild, crazy glint. He tossed the vibrator back down and stood. "Do it, then."

Swallowing, she accepted the hand he offered and stood, easing in closer until she was pressed against his chest, waiting. He grinned down at her, his hair falling into his face. "You wanted to kiss me stupid, baby girl. Have at it."

Cupping his face in her hands, she eased up onto her toes, angling her head just a little as she pressed her mouth to his. Hmmm. The way he tasted. He was...yeah. Just amazing. Just like his voice. Whiskey-soaked addiction. Flicking her tongue against his lips, she groaned as he opened for her. Leaning in closer, she nibbled on his lower lip, nipped the upper one and then pushed inside.

He shuddered against her, but remained unmoving, impassive.

If it wasn't for the way she could feel his chest rising and falling against her, so ragged and harsh, she might think he was unaffected. If it wasn't for the way his body felt rigid, heavy with tension and need, she might think he wasn't as aroused as she was.

One drugged kiss after another—now the need pulsed inside her, a vicious ache.

When she pulled away, she paused and rubbed her cheek against his, smiling at the way his unshaven skin rasped against the softness of her own. Shooting a quick look at his eyes, she shivered a little when she saw that he was watching her, his gaze so focused, so intense.

She pressed a kiss to his chin, down his neck. Along the sleek muscled lines of his chest. "You know, for a piano player, you sure are cut," she teased. "What do you do, lift the pianos or something?"

"I chase after smart-mouthed web designers," he muttered, swatting her on the ass.

"I don't think that would make you look quite like this," she said, sighing as she smoothed her hands over his chest. The silver hoop in his nipple was gone, replaced by a barbell. Tugging on it, she watched as a fine tremor racked his body. "I like this."

He cupped the back of her head in his hand, guided her mouth to his nipple.

She caught the bit of metal between her teeth, tugged on it again, a little harder this time, and satisfaction pulsed through her as he hissed out a breath.

Looking up at him, she saw that his head had fallen back, the thick black hair falling away from his face, eyes heavy lidded, mostly closed.

Going to her knees, she reached for his belt buckle, then unsnapped, unzipped his jeans. Tugging them down to just below his ass, she caught him in her hand, pumped once. Twice. Then she leaned in and licked him.

"Open your mouth," he growled, pushing his hand into her hair.

She did, just a little. Enough to lick his head. He bumped demandingly against her lips. "Open your mouth, Chaili. I want to see you with my cock in your mouth. I want to fuck that pretty mouth and I want it now."

Hunger was a beast in her belly as she did as he ordered, opening for him, her lips stretching wide as he pushed deep inside. He cupped her head between his hands and started to move, thrusting his cock in, out. She would have groaned if she could. Would have sighed. As it was, she couldn't stay still, the need was too much. Still cupping him in one hand, she reached down and circled her clit with her fingers.

"Don't," he warned. "You want this...you wanted to take me in your mouth, now do it. You can come later." He slowed, pulling back, until he'd pulled completely out.

She groaned, trying to follow, but he wouldn't let her. "Is that a problem?"

"No," she snarled, reaching for him again.

"Do you want me to come in your mouth?"

Her lashes flickered and she licked her lips. Hell, he just didn't have any hesitation, did he? "Yes."

"Good." This time, when she reached for him, he let her and he stroked deep into her mouth. Harder. Faster, until her eyes burned from it and her throat felt battered, but she loved it.

She went to let go of him again, her clit burning and tight.

"Don't you fucking dare touch yourself," he ordered. "That's for me, you hear?"

She whimpered around the cock in her mouth, but stopped, instead reaching up and gripping his thigh, her nails biting into his flesh. His groan sounded like it was torn out of him and his hands tightened in her hair. He pushed deep, held still.

Then, as he started to come, as her body screamed for

oxygen and its own release, she stared up at him. He was still watching her, those golden eyes hungry and hot.

She left him all but devastated. Drained. Empty. And ready to fill himself up with her. With everything she was.

As he let go of her hair, she eased back and remained where she was, on her knees, leaning in to press her cheek to his thigh. His cock twitched as he felt the soft caress of her breathing drift over him.

No. He wasn't empty, after all.

Urging her to her feet, he kissed her, reaching down to cup her in his hand, and he groaned as he felt how wet she was. "You like doing that."

"Yes…"

"How much?"

"Enough to want to do it again. And again."

She watched him with a lazy, lambent look in her eyes as he curved one hand over her hips.

"It's my turn now. On the bed. In the middle. Move back," he told her, closing his eyes, jerking himself under control. He wanted more than just a hot, erotic fuck with her. He wanted her to understand she was still beautiful…and he'd already realized that she didn't believe that anymore.

He wanted her to understand she was amazing.

He wanted to push her to the edge…and maybe let her take him there as well. He'd never danced to the line with anybody, but wouldn't mind going over it with her.

Stripping his jeans away, he kicked them off and draped them over the chair positioned by her bed. He'd already noticed she was pin neat about things. Wasn't going to clutter up the pretty little space she had. Moving to the bed, he picked up the scarf and moved closer, grabbing one ankle. "You've got a perfect bed," he said softly. "For this..."

The thick, black fringe of her lashes drooped down, shielding her eyes as he tied her left ankle to the bottom post of her bed. He checked, making sure she had plenty of room in case she jerked on it as she started to move. "Feel okay?'

She nodded, her breath coming in uneasy pants.

"Good." He slid a hand up her calf. "You have more of these scarves?"

"In my dresser," she whispered. "Bottom left drawer."

He left her lying there and returned with a handful of scarves, the pretty, colorful bits fluttering in his grip. He used a blue one on her right ankle. Two black ones on her wrists. As she was spread out, bound and open for him, he stood back to admire her.

He caught one more scarf, this one in bright, murder red and pushed it into her right fist. "I want to gag you," he said quietly. "Blindfold you. If you want me to stop, drop the scarf."

She shuddered, then nodded, clutching the scarf in her hand.

Two more scarves, one around her eyes, the other around her mouth, partly between her lips, her mouth open just enough, the scarf biting into her skin, just enough... "Too tight?"

She shook her head.

"Can you move much?"

She tried, tugging against the bonds.

Smiling, Marc said, "Good."

He took the vibrator, the one with the extension to tease her back entrance, and turned it on, watching her. She tensed. He turned it back off. Picked up the lubricant, checked it out.

Wasn't a kind he liked much, but he didn't care at that point. He'd use whatever he could if it meant he could do as he wanted with her.

"Seeing you like this..." he murmured, circling around to stand at the foot of the bed. He stared up at her, his gaze lingering between her spread thighs, along the flat plane of her belly, tracing the lines of her tattoo before moving up to her face. "I think I'll dream about this for a long, long time, Chaili. And I'll want to do this to you again and again."

He rested one knee on the mattress. "Is that okay?"

One slow nod. She angled her head and he smiled, suspected she was trying to see him under the scarf. He didn't care. It was all about setting the feel more than anything else. For now.

He sprawled between her thighs, leaving the vibrator and the lube on the bed next to her hip before sliding his hands under her ass. Lifting her up just a little, he blew a soft puff of air against her sex. She shuddered and groaned against the gag.

"I want to listen as you scream behind that scarf. I want to make you come. Then I'm going to push my cock into you and do it again. And again. I want to fuck your ass while you're on your knees. If you don't want that...you know how to make it all stop."

Her fingers clutched the scarf so tight, they were all but bloodless.

With a smile, he pressed his mouth to the hot, wet entrance of her pussy and licked her.

Chaili couldn't take much more of this.

But there was no way she was going to stop it. No way.

Still, as he settled his weight between her thighs, she was desperate for air. Desperate for a few seconds to rest. Just plain desperate.

"Shhh," he whispered, kissing her cheek, stroking his hands down her side, along her spine, soothing and gentle. The head of his cock butted against the mouth of her pussy. Two orgasms. Two mind-blowing orgasms and he was just now settling his weight on hers.

She was almost painfully sensitive now and the brush of his thumb against her clit was like the lash of lightening. She flinched and he eased back. "You know how to make me stop."

If she hadn't been tied spread eagle, she would have wrapped her arms and legs around him. Stop? Like hell. Instead, she arched against him. Twisted. Yearning.

No. She didn't want him stopping.

Chuckling, he rubbed his lips against her cheek, just above the edge of the scarf. "Okay, baby girl. That's good, because I still have things I want to do..."

As he pushed inside her, slowly, teasingly, she groaned, her head thrashing on the pillow. It was the one part of her body she could freely move, other than her hips—oh, yes. Her hips. Arching up, she tried to take him deeper, clenching down to milk him.

He growled and pushed down. "Be still," he ordered.

But she couldn't. Even as sensitive as she was, she was on fire for him. Aching. Desperate to be filled with him. She did it again and again...

He pulled out, his fingers biting into her hips. Surged back in. Deeper. Deeper. She sobbed against the gag, rising to meet him.

His breath came harsh, heavy. "Damn it, I wanted this

slow," he growled.

She didn't. She just wanted him. Needed him. So desperately.

The climax had been waiting, hiding just out of reach and as he slammed into her, it was there again. Taking her in greedy, gulping bites until she was falling...falling...

She felt him swell inside her and then he was gone, jerking at the bonds on her wrists until she could move her hands, jerking at the gag. She gasped for air and went to push away the blindfold but he was already moving, freeing her ankles and turning her around, onto her hands and knees. Then he had her hands bound, at the small of her back. When he pushed one of her other vibrators inside, sudden and without warning, she shrieked and arched upright, crying out.

His hand fisted in her hair. "You wanted me to be careful how hard I push you...you should be careful, Chaili. I'm trying to be nice here. I'm trying to take it easy and slow and you're about to break me. Bend over. I want that ass."

He didn't wait for her to bend, just nudged her down until she was facedown against her mattress, ass thrust up for him, while the vibrator twisted and wriggled inside her.

She shuddered, the sensation just too much, but she couldn't stop it and each time she thought the damn thing might wiggle and squirm its way free, he nudged it deeper. That was why she'd bought the damn thing. It was designed to stay lodged inside better than a regular vibrator, but damn it, this was just too—

"Marc," she gasped.

He was spreading the lubricant over her. Working it inside her ass. One finger thrusting in. Out. She flinched, jerking against the scarf he'd used on her wrists, clutching the one he'd given her as the signal if she needed to stop.

When he pushed a second finger, she almost dropped it. Not because she wanted him to stop, but because it was just too much. Too good, too hot, too erotic—

And then he stopped.

Just stopped.

Seconds ticked away.

Then he said quietly, "Are you ready, baby girl?"

"Yes." Hell. If she got any more ready, she was going to start begging him, and she hated that.

If he could turn back time...

No. Not now, he told himself as he settled on his knees behind her. He slicked his hand up his cock, the lubricant gleaming against his flesh. Holding himself steady, he pressed the head against the tight pucker of her ass and pressed.

The tight glove of her body resisted...at first, before flaring open around him, slowly, oh, so damned slowly, taking him in. Inch by slow inch.

With his free hand gripping the scarf that bound her wrists, he tugged her back just a little, watched as he sank into her. She was tight. Silken hot. Silken soft. Easing back, he waited until all but the flared tip had exited, and then he started the slow process all over again. Using his hips, and his grip on the scarf, to join them.

She whimpered and wiggled, tried to take him deeper.

Faster.

He spanked her, bringing his hand down on the taut, round flesh of her ass with resounding thoroughness. Just the sound of it made his balls draw tight against his body, but seeing that pink flush spread across her ass made his brain go all muzzy. "Be still," he said gruffly. "You try to take control away from me again and I'll stop. I'll come all over your ass and make you wait an hour before I let you climax."

"You fucking asshole," she rasped, twisting her hips and trying to take him deeper.

"See...now that's why we didn't use the word asshole as a safe word," he teased, surprised he was even able to laugh.

She groaned, her body trembling.

He stroked his fingers down her spine. "I'm going to make you come, Chaili. But first...I'm going to make you so fucking hot, so fucking ready..."

"I *am* ready."

"Not yet," he muttered.

No...net yet.

But she was close. Her flesh flushed pink. Her body shuddering. Trembling.

He went still, not moving at all, using just his grip on the scarf to move her, loving the tight glide of her over his cock, loving the sight of her bound hands and the way she shuddered and twisted and cried. Something fell against his thigh—the vibrator.

And still she was crying out, twisting and riding his dick like she couldn't get enough.

He tugged harder, started to rock again. Then he went from slow and lazy motions to deep, hard digs. She tensed and he looked, checked to make sure she was still gripping the scarf. Hot, hungry little mewls fell from her lips and although she'd stopped moving, her entire body quivered. It was like she was waiting—

Hunching over her, he let go of the scarf and rasped, "Now you're ready."

Sweat dripped from him and he started to fuck her in

126

earnest, so desperate and so hungry. She cried out his name in sudden, hungry shock and the sound of it was the most beautiful sound ever—better than the sound of his favorite Steinway in the middle of an empty concert hall, better than the chant of his name on the lips of a hundred thousand screaming fans.

Better than anything.

And as she started to come, he realized, that this...right here...this woman in his arms just might be everything.

Chapter Nine

She was sleeping.

Marc told himself he shouldn't be prying, but he'd showered. Made himself a peanut butter sandwich—he really hated peanut butter, but there wasn't much else and he wasn't leaving, so he made do.

He hadn't meant to pry exactly, but when he'd gone back into her room, just the sight of her hit him hard and that song that had been dancing in the back of his head for weeks, months...it just kind of exploded and he'd sat down to root around for some paper and accidentally knocked over some of the bills he'd noticed earlier.

It had been an accident.

Now he was stuck there, half sick with the bills she was still struggling to pay.

Shit, this didn't make sense. He had a dozen people who'd told him they loved his web design and they'd contacted his designer. She was the one who'd designed it, so why wasn't she able to cover these better?

Okay. It was something he'd figure out.

For now, he just had to...

"Hey."

Closing his eyes at the low, husky sound of her voice, he dropped the pen and blew out a breath. *Level out, Marc. Gotta level out now.* It didn't matter that he was half-sick thinking about what she'd been living with the past few years, and it didn't matter that his head all but wanted to come apart under the sheer, unimaginable weight of what she had to deal with on a daily basis.

All that mattered was that she was awake and they needed to get through the morning, have that talk he knew they needed to have...and he needed to do it without screwing it all up again.

And he wasn't going to be able to if he got all caught up in what he'd just discovered.

Picking up the lyrics he'd been working on, he turned around and smiled at her. It probably wasn't much of a smile, but he could blame that on the fact that he was hungry, that he needed coffee...and damn...

She sat there with the golden light streaming in through the faint slit in the curtains and he didn't think he'd ever seen anything more beautiful.

"Fuck, you're beautiful," he said gruffly.

He'd said that to other women. Most of them either blushed or smiled and said thank you.

Chaili sat there and snorted. "Whatever." She swung her legs over the edge of the bed and sat up, winding a sheet around her body. "What are you doing?"

He held up the piece of paper. "Music. Song's been eating at the back of my brain for a few months and it's finally coming free. Wanted to jot it down. I swiped a piece of paper."

"That's fine." She winked at him. "You can leave fifty cents on the table to cover it."

Crooking a grin at her, he folded the paper in half. "Fifty cents? Damn, paper is really going through the roof these days."

"Maybe it was a very important piece of paper." Rising from the bed, she came toward him, the sheet trailing after her, parting to reveal a long, leanly muscled thigh. He found himself staring at her leg, at the slit in the sheet where the cloth parted, wanting to tug it farther apart, see just a little. There was something almost painfully erotic, beautifully sexy about her clad in nothing but that white sheet. "Man, I bet you were a hit at toga parties in college."

Chaili laughed. "Sure I was. Half the jocks wanted to butter me up and see if they could get me to do their term papers for them. The others wanted to see if they could get in my pants." She reached out and trailed a finger down the sheet of paper. "Maybe I could let you have the paper for free...if you'd let me see what you're working on."

As the dull flush started to creep up his neck, he shrugged and passed it off. There weren't too many people he'd shared his stuff with early on, but Chaili had always been one of them. Unable to sit there casually while she read it, he reached for her, fisting his hands in the sheet and using it to tug her close. "We still need to have that talk," he said hoarsely. "I was kind of thinking about ordering some lunch in. Us having that talk. Or we can go out to my place and I can cook for you."

She lifted an eyebrow, a mocking smile on her lips. "I kind of value my stomach lining, sweetheart. I've had your cooking before. You burn macaroni and cheese."

"Hey." Swatting her on the ass, he tipped his head back, stared up at her. "I'll have you know I figured out how to cook. Had to, unless I wanted to live on take out or frozen pizza. I had a friend teach me."

"A friend, huh?" She went back to reading, the smile on her face softening. "This is going to be beautiful, Marc. One of your best."

"You think so?"

"Yeah." She gave it back to him and bent down, brushing

her lips against his. "As tempting as it is to spend the day with you, I need to get some work done. I had a new client contact me with a rush job and I need to at least get the design roughed out for her."

"Dinner, then." He continued to hold her waist even as she tried to turn away. "You can't go all day without a break, right? Besides, there's nothing here to eat besides peanut butter and ramen noodles."

"I'll have you know I love ramen noodles."

He gagged. "I don't know how you can say that with a straight face."

Well, she loved the price of them. She could stretch her money a hell of a lot further with stuff like peanut butter, ramen noodles, macaroni and cheese and pasta. Not exactly the healthiest diet, but it wouldn't last forever. She hoped. Shrugging, she said easily, "Hey, to each their own."

Tugging his wrists away from her hips, she headed over to her dresser. "I need to shower and get to work if we're going to do dinner."

She rummaged through her closet, wishing for the hundredth time there was something a little more *wow* to wear. A lot of her stuff she'd sold in yard sales or on eBay after it became clear that her body just didn't wear styles the way it used to. It would be nice, she thought wistfully, to have the money and go out, go shopping without worrying about price tags so much, without worrying about budgeting every last penny.

"Have you gotten much business your way from doing my site?"

She frowned, tugging a shirt off a hanger. "No. Not really." Of course, she hadn't been doing his site for well over two years

131

now. Weird time to ask her that, she mused, reaching for a wrap skirt. She'd made that herself, solid black, and paired with the bright, splashy fabric of the shirt she'd picked out, it softened the long, lean lines of her body, gave her a little more feminine look.

"Huh. Sorry. I woulda thought...well. Never mind."

She turned around, saw him sitting there at the desk, running the sheet of paper through his hands. Back and forth. Dragging his thumb and forefinger down the crease. Turn it. Down the edge. Turn it. Down the crease. He looked...blue, she decided. Something about the way he sat there, head down, shoulders slumped.

"You know, I've had fantasies about those hands of yours."

She watched as his hands stilled, watched as he lifted his head just a little and stared at her through his lashes.

A hungry light glinted in his eyes. "I thought you needed to get a jump on work," he said gruffly.

"I do. I just wanted to mention that." Grinning at him, she brushed by him, paused by her dresser for a pair of panties and then headed out to the hallway.

Just before she left the room, she glanced back at him and saw that he was watching, still with that hot, hungry look on his face. "So we're doing dinner?"

"Yes."

Marc waited until the shower came on.

Then he turned back to the desk.

She was going to kick his ass for this, but damn it, the sheer magnitude of the medical debt she had was killing him. He remembered, damn well, what it was like to pinch pennies, scrape together just enough to pay the bills, to try and figure which ones it was okay to skip for a few weeks and which ones had to be paid.

He also knew why she was living on ramen noodles and peanut butter. He'd done the same damned thing. And why in the hell wasn't she getting some business from doing his website? He had a fucking awesome site, and it was because of her, although he wasn't too hot on some of the updates that had been done on it the past year or so.

Maybe he'd talk to her about that. In a few days. Nice and casual like. Tell her he wanted something different and offer a bonus or something if she got it done by a certain date... She seemed really big on meeting deadlines, so if he offered her a bonus?

Something to cover some of these bills?

He studied them. Shit, she'd see through him in a heartbeat if he covered them all.

But he'd figure out something.

Once he'd committed the figures to memory, the doctor's offices to memory, he left her bedroom and went to the living room. It served as her office too, the sleek, powerful computer set-up in the corner the one thing that was clearly *not* set up with budget in mind. It was all power, all efficiency and workhouse.

He booted it up and went to his website, thinking about making a few notes.

But then he felt like somebody had kicked him in the chest.

Down at the bottom was something he hadn't noticed before.

Website maintained by BG Enterprises.

What the mother fucking...

Hissing out a breath, he clicked away from the website as

he heard the shower go off. She wasn't doing his site anymore.

Damn it.

He knew that had been a decent chunk of her income. She'd once even teasingly mentioned to him that she needed to start sending him a better Christmas gift, since he was her number one client.

How in the hell had this happened?

And who in the *fuck* was BG Enterprises?

"Who in the fuck is BG Enterprises?"

Not entirely sure his manager would get to it in a timely manner since they were on a break, Marc had called the one person he knew would get him the info. Ilona.

"It's your website design company, I believe," she said, yawning into the phone. "Marc, buddy, you do remember, you're supposed to be on vacation. And normally, when *you* are on vacation, I get a bit of a vacation too, right?"

"Screw the vacation. How in the hell do they get to be my website company? And they didn't design it. That's Chaili's design. They just tacked a bunch of cheap-ass shit on top of her design. And it *sucks*, by the way. Fire them. Hire her back. Wait. We can't just do it like that..." Sitting in his car, parked in the garage, he dropped his head against the steering wheel. The first time didn't do anything to inspire a genius method of handling this, so he did it again.

But by the fourth hit, genius still hadn't attacked and his head was hurting. "Okay, Ilona. I need to find out what happened. How they ended up doing the job *I* hired *her* to do years ago. And she was doing a damned good job of it."

"I can answer some of that," Ilona said. "But you're going to be pissed."

"I'm already pissed. When did it happen?"

"Two years ago." Off in the background there was a clatter, and then she said, "Give me a minute."

He all but bit through his tongue to demand answers, listening to her talking in a low, soft voice. Her kid. She had a child from a previous marriage, a girl that Miguel adored. The clattering continued for a few more seconds while he continued to think. The answer came to him abruptly.

"Lily."

The clattering cut off almost as soon as he said it and Ilona said softly, "Yes. Lily. She'd emailed me about getting some stuff added to your site, so I emailed Chaili, the way we always did, although I wanted to talk to you because a lot of it was big-time stuff. You told me to talk it over with Chaili. She knew what worked for you and what didn't. We were in Tokyo at the time. Chaili ended up emailing me... I think Lily was being a bitch to her but she was as nice as she's always been, told me some of the stuff you were asking for just wasn't going to work well with your current website design but if you wanted it, she could do it. It would just take a website redesign. It would be a few months to get everything completed."

"And you told her...?"

"I said not to worry about what Lily was griping about. You'd let Chaili know if the site needed an overhaul. Two months later, the site was taken over by BG Enterprises."

"And you didn't point this out to me because...?"

There was a pause. "Marc...I did. I emailed you about it twice, and you didn't answer. I called you about it and asked if things were cool with you and Chaili, and you didn't seem to know what in the hell I was talking about. I asked about the website, and you said, and I quote, *'I have you and Lily to handle that shit for me, remember?'* So I asked if you were aware of the changes with the website and you said, *'Not too crazy with the photo shit, but if that's what people want, fine.'* Then you hung up on me."

Somewhere in the back of his mind, the vague memory bumped free and if it were possible, he would have kicked his own ass. He would have done it, and done it happily. "You weren't calling about the stupid photo gallery, were you?"

"Nope. I was trying to tell you somebody else had taken over the site and done a shitty job of it." She sighed. He could practically see her shoving her hand through her hair, tugging at it the way she did when he'd done something that had her *really* frustrated. "I take it you just now figured it out, didn't you?"

"Yes. I need Chaili back doing my site, Ilona. But I need it done in a way that's not going to look..."

"Ham-handed?" she offered.

"Yeah." Shoving open the door, he headed around the back and popped the trunk. He grabbed as many of the groceries bags as he could, one-handed. He'd make a trip for the rest of them in a minute. "I want a total redesign. Tell her we've just been unhappy with the current company or something and I want to go back to the way I used to have the site, but with a more modern feel or something like that."

"Maybe you should talk to her," Ilona said.

"If I talk to her, she's going to figure out something is up."

"Something *is* up, damn it," Ilona snapped. "You're pushing work her way, aren't you?"

"No!" Groaning, he juggled the bags and managed to get the key in, pausing to disarm the alarm system before making his way into the kitchen. Why in the hell was the kitchen on the other side of the house? "Yes. Not exactly...fuck. Look, my website looks like shit now. The idiot doing it has it looking like a garage band. It might have been okay for us ten years ago, but it's not now. I need a better site. It looked better when Chaili did it and you know it. I want her doing it again."

"Then why can't you just tell her that?" Ilona said reasonably. "Look, if I'm the one doing this, she's going to wonder why you didn't bring it up. Just tell her the crazy bitch you stupidly hired on as a manager fired her with no input from you. And you, being who you are, just now figured it out. Chaili knows how you are, right? She'll understand. Tell her you want her handling the website again. What's going to cause the problem?"

The images of those bills flashed in front of his eyes.

Sighing, he dumped the bags on the counter. "If you were her, how would you feel about it?"

"Well, it wouldn't happen."

He scowled. "What?"

"You two are screwing, right?"

Marc passed a hand over his face. "Ilona, you're such a romantic. I don't know how Miguel can possibly hope to keep you happy, considering what a soft, poetical-type heart you have."

"Ha! I knew it. And that's why it wouldn't happen. Marc, you're hotter than hell and if I wasn't married to Miguel and shit-faced in love with him, I might have a few wet dreams about you, except...well. I know you. You either frustrate the hell out of me, or you freak me out. And if it wasn't *that* getting in the way? I'd have to deal with the crazy bitches who always manage to find their way into your life. So...it wouldn't happen. But..." She sighed. "Chaili's known you most of your life, right? You're probably more of a real person to her."

"I am a real person," he said sourly.

"Not to a lot of people," Ilona said quietly. "They put you on a pedestal and worship you. And when you don't act like the god they think you are, they demonize you. Chaili just sees you. I just see you. That's not a bad thing, pal. Look, I get what you're asking and I suspect Chaili is having some money problems otherwise you wouldn't be all gung ho to get this done *now*. But this isn't complicated. She did a kickass job on the site before and you want her handling it again. Just whatever you do...*don't go giving her handouts*. That's *not* good."

Scowling, he stared at the groceries. He'd almost bought some stuff for her place. Thinking about those mostly bare shelves had pissed him off. Bothered him. Badly. "What's a handout?"

"Giving her money. Paying her bills. That sort of thing."

He groaned. Paying off her damn medical bills was exactly what he wanted to do. That, and maybe buy her some fucking groceries...but he couldn't do that, either.

"Okay, so if I hire her and like offer bonuses and shit, that's fine, right?"

"Yes." Ilona sighed, but there was something mocking, teasing in the sound. "You see, you're expecting her to work for it, right? You're not going to hire her to do a job and then think it's okay to let her do a crappy one and still pay her, right?"

Heading back out the garage, he grabbed the rest of the bags. "You've seen her work, right? Chaili—she's the perfectionistic type who sent me like twenty different mockups before we settled on the last redesign? She doesn't *do* crappy."

"Okay, then. You're hiring her to do a job and you're expecting her to do the job, right?"

"Of course I am." Kicking the door shut behind him, he dumped the rest of the bags on the counter. Maybe he'd make extra. If he made extra and just bitched about hating to have leftovers or something...that could maybe work...

"Now you're following. Paying her to do a job she's capable of is different from just giving her money."

Rubbing the heel of his hand over his chest, he turned and stared out over the water.

"How bad are things?" Ilona asked, her voice hesitant.

"Bad. But this is between us."

She sighed. "I figured that much. Good luck...you can do this. You aren't anywhere near as lousy with talking to people as you used to be. And when they matter, you're usually pretty decent."

Decent, he thought, shoving the phone into his pocket.

That wasn't enough for Chaili.

She deserved more than *decent.*

Chapter Ten

With her gym bag, a spare set of clothes and her laptop stowed in the back of Marc's car, Chaili rested her elbow on the door and studied the man behind the wheel.

He was nervous, edgy about something. He'd been that way ever since he picked her up, but now that they were in the car, it was worse. Her heart twisted as she tried to figure out the cause behind his nerves. Was he tired of this already?

That didn't seem right.

If for no other reason than because her heart was still in overtime from the kiss he laid on her when he picked her up ten minutes earlier.

But something had him worked up.

If there was any one thing she knew about Marc, it was that he *moved*.

He was never still.

When he drove, his hands tapped out a beat on the steering wheel. He paced. He sat at his piano and played.

When he was still, it was because he was thinking, nervous...or pissed.

As they made the drive to his place, it seemed as though all that wild, chaotic energy had been sucked inside him. She didn't think he was pissed. So he was either nervous...or thinking about something really hard.

If he was thinking, whatever it was had to be pretty heavy. He clutched at the steering wheel so tightly his knuckles had gone bloodless. Smoothing down her skirt, she crossed her legs and tried to figure out if she should ask him what was up or just let it go.

Maybe—

"I need to ask you something. It's not personal, but I'm probably going to blunder and fuck it up, so can you cut me slack when I do?" he asked, shooting her a look before checking the mirror and cutting over into the next lane of traffic.

Chaili propped her head on her hand, eyeing him narrowly. "You know, you never used to worry so much about blundering with me. What's the deal?"

"I wasn't fucking you before," he muttered. "It's a little bit different after I've had your sweet pussy around my dick. Because now I'm worried I'm going to piss you off and I won't get to have it again."

Stifling her groan, she clenched her thighs together. "Well, you've already pointed out it's not personal, so I assume it's not about us having sex, right?"

"No." He started to beat his fist on the door. "It's about my website. Why in the hell didn't you tell me you weren't working on it anymore?"

Something twisted in her belly. Absently, she toyed with the fringe on her wrap skirt. Anything to keep from looking at him. Hell, when she'd lost that account, it had almost gutted her, and not because of how she felt about him. That had been the biggest chunk of her income and if she hadn't lost that account...well, she had. It didn't matter.

"What do you mean why didn't I tell you?" she asked. "It's your site. Why should I tell you what's going on with your site?"

"Because I didn't know," he said, his voice sour. "My ex-manager, Lily, is the idiot who did all of that. I just figured it out when I was checking something on the page. I wanted to talk to you about some updates and shit and I noticed the logo down at the bottom. It ain't yours. And the damn site sucks. I should have figured it out before now. Why in the hell didn't you say anything?"

One of the many knots, one of those ever-present aches that had been in her chest, unclenched...unfolded. He hadn't dumped her. Yeah, it wasn't a break-up, but she'd felt like she let him down when he stopped using her service and it had hurt. Badly.

Swallowing, she shrugged. "It was a business thing, Marc. I just figured you knew." Hell, Lily had *told* her Marc knew about it. Her words... *Marc knows he needs a little more...sophistication in his designer, but he doesn't want to hurt your feelings. Look, we can be grown-up about this or you can continue to cling to him. It's your call.*

"I didn't fucking know."

"You swear too much, slick," she told him, fighting the urge to squirm in the seat. Lily had lied to her. Lied to her and cost her the biggest account she had, made her feel like a fool...of course, she'd been so tired and sick at the time—the chemo had been taking its toll.

Closing her eyes, she pressed her hand to her forehead, trying to think past the headache creeping up on her.

"What the fuck does it matter how much I swear?" he demanded. He shot up the exit ramp and then had to hit the brakes to avoid ramming the car in front of them. "Why didn't you talk to me about this?"

"Because I thought you knew what was going on," she said again. "It's your website. You've always kept a hand in things and I thought you knew."

"I'm telling you I didn't. Hell, it's still your design." He paused and then said, "Your design but it looks awful."

"Yes." She smiled, crossing her arms over her chest. "It does. The idiots doing it don't know what in the hell they're doing. They're trying to smash a bunch of shit together with no idea whether or not it works together, and it's lousy."

"You're taking it back over."

She slid him a sideways look. "You know, generally when somebody wants to use my services, they put in a request. Ask for a quote. Give me an idea of what they want and then we talk it out and see if we can come to an agreement."

He grunted. "You already know the sort of style I like, but the entire thing needs to be trashed. I'd rather you just put a placeholder thing up—whatever they call it—and start from scratch. And if you get it done within a decent amount of time, I'll even throw in a bonus. I'm tired of looking at that eyesore."

"A bonus?" she asked. Narrowing her eyes, she studied him. "How much of a bonus?"

"Shit. I dunno." He drummed his fingers on the wheel as the car edged up the ramp. Finally, he was able to turn and as they took off down the road, he named a figure that almost had her jaw dropping.

"Are you *serious*?"

That...what... Damn it. She licked her lips. "Marc, that's a little steep for a bonus."

It would take care of a few of those bills, she thought, dazed. Not all of them, but a couple of them. She could maybe stop living on peanut butter and ramen noodles.

She could buy some new clothes...

And she'd be taking advantage of him. "That's too much for doing a job you're going to pay me for anyway," she said, her voice weaker than she'd like to admit. Damn it, she needed that money.

"Not if you get it done in the time frame I need it. We start working on the new CD in six weeks and I'd like to be able to post updates and stuff to the website. I keep getting told I need to update how the social media shit plays into the website and I figure you can do that too. I can't do anything with that disaster of a site I've got now. If you can get it done in time to launch it in...maybe five weeks?"

"Five *weeks*?" she squeaked out.

She thought it through—she could do it. She'd have to work it in around her current workload, but if she didn't accept any other projects in the meantime and if she stayed up a little later...maybe. Maybe. And assuming he was a little more communicative than he normally was when it came to this sort of thing. "Ah, you said you want it redesigned. Just what did you have in mind? And are you going to be around for me to show the ideas to? I can't send you fifty emails and wait days for answers."

His hand curved over her thigh and her breath skittered out of her lungs as he squeezed. "Oh, I'm going to be around plenty," he said, his voice a low, sexy growl. He glanced down at her skirt, eyed it and then grinned, flipped it open and slid his hand up, up, up...*ahhhh.* She gasped as he pulled her panties aside and flicked his finger over her clit.

"Weren't we talking...um...business stuff?"

"Yes." He grinned, his teeth flashing at her. "You're doing the website. I'm paying you a chunk of change to get it done fast. Business talk done... We can talk personal stuff now. I'm going to play with you until you come right there in that seat."

Chaili clutched at the armrest, turning her head and staring blindly out the window. They were speeding down the road, but by no means were they the only car out there. "Damn it, Marc, other people can see..." She shuddered as he circled

144

her entrance.

"Hmmm. Should I stop?"

As he went to pull his hand away, she grabbed his wrist. "No."

Blood rushed hotly to her cheeks.

"Pull your panties down," he said.

She swallowed, looking around.

"Nobody is paying attention, Chaili. The windows are tinted. Besides you'd have to be in a truck or something to really see in and be able to tell what you're doing...what I'm going to do." He pulled his hand away, slowly, his fingers trailing over her thigh. "But if you don't want to take them off..."

Groaning, she wiggled around until she could hook her fingers in the waistband of her panties, lifting her hips as much as the seatbelt would allow, working them down. Once she had them off, she went to stuff them in her purse but Marc held out his hand. "I want them."

She glared at him.

He continued to wait patiently.

Swearing, she pushed her panties into his hand. "We still haven't had that talk," she mumbled.

"Have I done anything outside your limits?"

"No." She almost wished she could say otherwise—wished she could maintain a little bit of distance between them, just to protect herself, because it would be that much easier when the end came, but she couldn't. It was like she had no brakes with him.

"You know what will make me stop, right?"

Chaili nodded, biting her lip and sinking back into the seat. When he pushed the panel of her skirt aside, she hissed out a breath.

Marc smiled, his lids drooping. "You're so damned wet for me. I love it."

A truck blasted by.

She sat up straight, squeezing her legs together, and then gasped as it pushed Marc's fingers deeper inside. "Oh," she whimpered.

"Hmmm. Chaili...I want to listen to you come."

He stroked her, whispering to her all the while. And the entire time, he drove on down the road, navigating through traffic like he wasn't screwing his fingers in and out of her pussy. "Ride my hand," he growled. "Take what you need."

She cried out, clenching her thighs around him, and rocked up, pushing one hand between her legs and stroking her clit, mindless for want of him.

"That's it, baby...come for me."

She came apart and it was pure torture not to watch.

But listening to her, feeling it, was a sweet seduction of its own.

She was panting, still gasping for breath a few minutes later when they pulled onto the road that led to his house. Those last few minutes had flown by in a blur and now all he wanted to do was get her to his place so he could have her.

The hard part had gone by easier than he'd thought.

He had a feeling Chaili wasn't telling him something, but he was going to bide his time there. Once she started the work and he paid her some money upfront, he'd probably pry a little. But he wanted her comfortable enough to start working on the site first.

He'd feel better once he had her at his place, in his bed...

But that fucking talk.

"You're bad for me," Chaili muttered.

Stiffening, he shot her a look and saw that she was staring at him from under her lashes, a smoky smile on her lips. "Yeah?"

"Hmmm. I don't think when I'm around you." She smoothed her palms down her thighs, then up, dragging the silky fabric of the skirt up. "And I'm fine with that."

"Thinking is overrated. Open your skirt." He glanced around. Nobody. His house was in sight now too. He looked over at her, watched as she eased the panel of her skirt aside, revealing the neat curls between her thighs. He could see the gleam of wetness there, the pink of her sex. "I'd like to pull over and fuck you right here. But too many cars pass by. Public sex isn't my thing."

She laughed, the sound shaky and soft. "Good. It's not really mine, either." Then she caught her lip between her teeth. "Although I can get into watching..."

"Watching, huh?"

He hit the brakes just before he would have shot past his house. "Damn it, you're the one who is bad for the brain." He hit the control for the garage and pulled in. "We stay here until we talk because otherwise, I'll have my dick inside you in five seconds once we're out of the car," he said bluntly, turning the car off and hitting the button to lower the garage door.

"Okay..." She stared at him, her lashes low, a feline smile curving her lips.

"One thing...what's this about watching?"

She laughed. "Well, the whole story might piss you off. You really want to hear?"

"Yes."

The ruby on her ring glinted at him as she pushed a hand

through her hair. "It's how Tim and I ended up...discovering our compatibilities. I think he knew I was into rough stuff, or was figuring it out. But we were at a party. I'd gone outside for some air. Somebody was smoking pot and I couldn't stand the smell of it. While I was outside, I heard...interesting noises." She slid him a sly look and then shrugged. "I followed. Saw a couple of people from the party having a very fun time indeed. And me, being the pervert that I am, stood there, enthralled. Tim came up behind and I was..."

She stroked a hand across her belly, eased it lower. "Very turned on. He figured it out. He didn't say anything but on our next date, he took me to a club."

"A club..." Shit. "Blue's," he said quietly.

She slanted a look at him. "Yeah. How come I'm not surprised you know about that place?"

"You..." He blew out a breath, told himself he wasn't going to be stupid with this. Okay, so Chaili had been going to the same fucking sex club he used. He'd seen Tim around there in the years since Chaili's divorce, but...okay. Dots connected.

"You've been to Blue's," he said slowly.

"Yeah. Seeing as how you already know it's a sex club that caters to the kinky crowd, I don't need to explain. I...uh...well, I didn't figure that out until we were already inside. He paid for access and took me to the voyeur rooms. Asked me if I liked what I saw...and then he yanked my skirt up."

Jealousy ripped through him as she bluntly said, "It was the best sex we'd ever had."

"So you like watching."

Chaili shrugged. "Sometimes. It was a thing with him. We'd been sleeping together and it wasn't bad. Just wasn't...amazing. But after that night, it was better. We were good for a while. We got married. Then he started pushing more. Seemed to think

148

the harder he pushed the better things would get. It didn't. Then..." She reached up, touched her chest.

Although he couldn't see it, he knew she was tracing the lines of her tattoo. "Then you found out about the cancer."

"You know, your sister is the entire reason I found the damn lump," she said quietly, staring straight ahead, looking at the windshield like it held the answer to life itself. "She'd just had a friend diagnosed...young, like me. I was annoyed with her, because she was constantly yapping about how young women can get cancer too. Breast cancer hits twelve percent of us. It gets *twelve percent* of us, you know that? But it only gets the older women—I was safe until I turned forty. That's what I thought. She said something over lunch...*do you do those exams, Chaili?* I told her *no.* She kept yammering at me. I thought I was safe," she whispered again. "But I wasn't. I told her I'd do the stupid thing if she'd leave me alone."

She licked her lips and lowered her hands, twisted them in her laps. "I went home to get to work on somebody's project. It was actually a website for a local young survivor's group. Fitting, huh? I was putting up a few pictures and suddenly, I just got up, went into the bathroom and took off my shirt. My bra. And I felt it. It was so small, didn't seem like it should be a big deal."

She was crying now, silent tears rolling out of her pretty eyes. "I even asked Tim what he thought, but he didn't even want to mess with it. It kind of freaked him out. Grossed him out too, if you want the truth. I made an appointment...had to do the mammogram and everything. And all the while, I kept telling myself it wasn't anything to worry about."

Leaning across the console, he hooked his arm around her neck, hugging her to him. "Chaili, fuck. I didn't mean to bring this up."

She laughed. "You didn't. I did. I didn't have to go there, it just sorta...I dunno. I think I'm more screwed up over some of this than I thought."

As she turned her face into his neck and breathed him in, he closed his eyes. *Don't let me screw this up.* That was all he wanted. Just that. Well, that and her. He was starting to think he wanted her forever, and he had to be careful not to mess this up.

Stroking a hand up her back, he cupped her nape, pressed a kiss to her cheek. "Come on. Let's go inside, have a glass of wine."

"No. I shouldn't. I try not to drink much...it's not good for me." She lifted her head to smile at him, pressed her brow to his. "Besides, we're supposed to have that all-important talk, remember? So you can fuck me as soon as we're out of the car."

He closed his eyes. Stroked her back. "I think I need the wine. Or a beer. Or a bottle of bourbon," he muttered, rubbing his knuckles up and down her spine. She gutted him. Laid him low. The hell she'd gone through...and he'd never known.

He stood in the kitchen, head bowed, an amber bottle in one hand, the other rubbing the back of his neck. She should have kept her mouth shut, Chaili thought morosely. "You want to do dinner another night?" she asked softly.

"No. I want to turn back time and wring your neck for not telling me this three years ago," he said bluntly, lifting his head and shooting her a dark look. He lifted the bottle to his lips and took a long drink, then set it on the counter with a heavy thunk. "But that's not anything we can change, right? And if I'd been around more..."

"Why weren't you?" The second she asked, she wished she

could yank the argument back. "Never mind. That's none of my business—"

"Lily. My old manager." He shrugged, a jerky, uneasy motion that said he was a hell of a lot more uncomfortable talking about this than his tone let on. "Her. Another ex-girlfriend before that. Seemed like any time I was here for longer than a few weeks, I got in trouble so I decided I wouldn't mess with it. It wasn't just here, though. It was any time I tried to settle in, so I just stopped trying to settle in. And now I'm kicking my ass for doing it. But shit, I was doing that before now. I missed my sister, I missed you, missed my friends..."

I missed you... Those words hit her. Hard and fast, like he'd punched her. But there was no pain. Just the shock. The surprise.

And it must have shown on her face, because he'd stopped talking and was staring at her. Frustrated too.

Chaili blinked, looking away from him. Now this was just perfect. She'd gone and gotten all emotional. Wasn't that just lovely?

"Chaili," he rasped, the growl of his voice stroking over her skin. "Now what did I do?"

"Nothing." She licked her lips and shrugged, feeling like a fool. "You just said you'd missed me, okay? You...I've missed you too."

There was a pause. Then she heard the soft scuff of his shoes over the tile as he crossed the floor to her. From the corner of her eye, she glanced at him and her breath hitched in her chest. "Did you now?" he murmured, caging her in, one arm on either side of her body.

"Yes." She turned her head to face him, shivering as he rubbed his stubbled cheek against her. Trying to lighten the moment, she said teasingly, "How could I not? After all, I never get to hear you sing anymore."

A grin crooked the corners of his mouth upward. "So it's all about the singing, huh?"

"Nah. Well." She pursed her lips and added, "Maybe a little. You do bad things to me when you sing, Marc."

"Hmm. Maybe I'll do more singing for you...just you." He leaned in and nipped her ear. "We need to have that talk, though, baby girl. Why don't we do it while I finish up dinner?"

"Why don't we do it now...and have dinner later?" She stared at him and stroked a hand down his chest, over the flat plane of his belly. It made her smile inwardly as she felt the muscles jump, then bunch under her hand. But before she got to his belt buckle, he caught her wrist.

"Talk, Chaili. Dinner. Then bed," he said gruffly. Thick black lashes shielded the gold of his eyes and then he looked at her, his brow pressed to hers. "I need a few minutes to level out, baby. Okay?"

A few minutes. A few hours. A few years.

He'd make do with the time he had between now and the end of the meal, but he had to get himself under control and he had to do it fast. Pressing a quick kiss to her lips, he pulled away and headed over to the fridge where the lasagna was waiting. "Everything's mostly done—just have to cook the lasagna and while that's going, we can do a salad, get the bread in the oven," he told her. "You sure you don't want some wine?"

She made a face at him. "I'd rather have sex, but you won't give me that." Sighing, she settled on a stool at the center island and crossed her legs, reminding him she was deliciously naked under that sexy skirt of hers. "I don't drink much. I can't. Well, theoretically, I shouldn't. I'm genetically predisposed to cancer. Drinking too much is tempting fate. So I don't."

Genetically— "What the fuck does that mean?" he asked hoarsely, dropping the glass pan of lasagna down on the counter before he hurled it across the kitchen.

Silence reigned.

Turning around, he stared at her. "What the hell does *genetically predisposed* mean?"

Her eyes narrowed. "Watch it, Marc," she warned quietly. "I don't much care to have people yelling at me unless I did something to warrant it. And guess what? *I didn't.*"

"I can't help it," he bit off. "Would you just fucking answer me? What does that mean?" Was he going to lose her right when he'd just found her? Is that what she was saying?

Long, tense moments ticked by before she finally looked away. "My genes are a little screwy. It's complicated, and if you want a better explanation, you'd be better off asking my doctor. But I was born with genes that make me a higher risk for breast cancer—which we didn't know about until they found it. Drinking a lot of alcohol can increase the risk. So I keep it to a glass of wine every once in a while."

"Will it come back?"

She glanced down, then shrugged and smiled. "There's not much for it to come back to. It's not *likely*. But cancer is an ugly, brutal bitch. We never know when she'll come back to give you a nice little sucker punch. That's why I don't tempt fate."

He sucked in a breath, blew it back out. A brutal, ugly bitch. Damn it. That was wording it mildly. Okay. He was trying to level out. Although it was damn hard, considering he kept getting one hit after another. It was like every time he thought he'd heard the hardest thing, seen the hardest thing, accepted the roughest thing, he was given another slap that sent him spinning, careening out of control.

Grabbing the lasagna pan, he went over to the stove and let

153

it drop down on it with a clatter as he turned the oven on.

"You keep banging that thing around, we won't be eating it. The pan's going to break," Chaili said from behind him.

"Nah. I bought stuff that's supposed to be pretty resistant," he said, striving for some light, easy ground.

"Resistant to you slamming them around? Designed with Marc in mind?"

He smiled, but it was half-hearted at best.

Turning around, leaning against the counter, he stared at her. "I'm having a hard time finding level ground here, just so you know. I'm probably going to hit my asshole level at some point soon tonight," he warned her.

She shrugged, toying with the fringe on her skirt. "You probably weren't expecting such a mess when you decided you wanted to...hell. What *are* we doing here, Marc?" The thick strands of her hair fell into her eyes and she brushed them back impatiently as she studied him. "What is this? Are you just looking for somebody to keep you company while you're on a break? Is..."

Her voice trailed off and she looked away.

But he saw the way her shoulders rose, fell, erratic, in time with the harsh sounds of her breathing before she steadied it out.

"You're asking me questions I don't have answers for," he said quietly. He pushed off the counter and moved to stand in front of her. Cupping her cheek in his hand, he stared down at her. "Relationships and me have about as much luck as a junkie trying to quit cold turkey. But then again, I haven't ever met a single woman who made me *want* any sort of real relationship." He dragged his thumb over her lower lip, watched as her pupils flared. "Until you. You drive me crazy in so many ways."

154

The oven beeped and he sighed, turned away and headed over to the oven, put the lasagna in.

"So."

He decided he'd stay just where he was for now. It was safer. "So."

They stared at each other and finally, Chaili slid off the stool and went over to the fridge, tugged it open, studied the contests before pulling out a can of Diet Coke. "Is that what we're doing, Marc? Going to try and have a relationship?"

"I thought we already were." He slid a hand into his pocket, rubbed a finger over the picture he had tucked in there. All those years he'd spent wasted on women who'd left him empty and the one he needed was right there. Right here. "Is that what you want?"

"Well..." She slanted a look at him, a wicked smile curving her lips. "I guess we can do a relationship. The sex is pretty fucking awesome."

Marc pulled the picture out, tapped his finger with it. Wondered maybe if he should try to press. She had a habit of doing that, he noticed. He'd try to push for deeper things, a deeper connection and she'd make it all light and easy.

Nothing he felt about her was light and easy.

But if she needed to keep it that way for now, that was fine. He glanced down at the picture and then slipped it back in his pocket. "I'm here to please you," he murmured. "And speaking of which..." He checked the timer.

Plenty of time.

"About that talk."

Chaili's heart stuttered in her chest as he caught her wrist and led her out of the kitchen. They went into the living room, but instead of stopping at the couch, he led her over to the upright Steinway he had against one wall.

"What, do I get one of those private concerts now?"

He just smiled and sat down, resting his hands on the keys. "You said you like to watch...is this a regular thing for you?"

Chaili groaned, blood creeping up her neck to turn her cheeks hot. "Yeah, sure. It's regular. I've got weekly dates at the local sex club just so I can watch people screw."

"I'm asking serious questions," he said quietly. "Serious answers would be nice."

A soft, easy piece started to fill the room and she sighed as she settled down next to him. If only she had something to do with *her* hands while he played. "No. It's not a regular thing. Hell, I don't *have* a regular thing, okay? It's not like I can only climax if you're giving me orders or holding me down or spanking me. It's just something..." She shrugged. "Hell, it's not even a thing I'm into anymore." Twisting the ring she wore around on her finger, she stared off into the distance. "I'm not the person I used to be. The things I used to think about, want...they've changed. I haven't thought about that in years."

"So it's not anything you need anymore?"

She closed her eyes and rested her head in her hands.

"It's not a hard question," he murmured.

Wasn't it? "Hell, Marc. I never *needed* it. It was just...a thing. Yeah, I liked it, but I didn't *need* it. The other stuff..." She licked her lips. "I think it would depend. Tim started trying to do the hardcore dom stuff. He'd bark out orders during sex and I loved that, loved being spanked and tied up. I'm inclined to submit during sex. That's just me. But he tried to take more than I wanted to give...wanted me to call him Master, and he'd tried to do the dom shit all the time..."

Marc gave a derisive snort. "He's been watching too many bad movies or reading too many bad books. If he's a real dominant, he'll take his cues from what his woman needs." He slid her a look. "I don't want to be called anything but my name."

"So I can't call you baby? Sweetheart?" She leaned in and pressed her lips to his arm, whispered, "Sugar...lover..."

He laughed. "That's not so much a problem. But I don't want to hear Master or any of that."

"Not your thing?"

Marc shrugged. "Not so much. I like what I like, but that doesn't mean I want to be anybody's master." He glanced at her, his hands still moving over the keys. "How deep did you go with it?"

"Tim wanted to go pretty damn deep." She shrugged. "He couldn't ever get me involved as much as he wanted, though. And with that kind of thing, it's got to be mutual. He wanted a devoted slave, and I'm not ever going to be that. I'll never call a man Master. He was getting seriously into it too. Was trying to talk me into doing contracts and shit, said we should have done a *collaring* ceremony instead of getting married." She paused and reached for his beer, lifted it to her lips. "Son of a bitch."

Marc laughed. "I guess you don't want to wear a collar."

"No." She thunked the bottle down on the seat and got up. "I've got a kinky streak and it's pretty damn wide. He started to yap about how he just needed to take a firmer hand with me. That if we'd just establish some ground rules, things would become more...*natural*. I was testing my limits and I just needed a master who understood me and that once I was taken in hand..." She curled her lip. "I told him the day he tried to take me in hand was the day I'd *break* his hands."

Tim had thought she was joking. She hadn't been. She'd

play the punishment game, and damn well any other game...on her terms. Sighing, she crossed her arms over her chest and looked back at him. "If you're that far into the lifestyle, we probably need to call it quits here, Marc. I play at it. But I won't ever do more than dance around the edges of it and I'll admit that. I don't *want* to live it and heaven help the man who thinks I'll address him as Master just because I prefer to get topped during sex."

"That happened?"

"Shit, what is this, twenty questions?" Scooping her hair out of her face, she shrugged. "Yes. We went to the club and Tim made the mistake of introducing me as his slave. His first mistake. Because I never *agreed* to be anybody's slave. A few of the guys he knew seemed to think that meant I'd call *them* Master. I informed them otherwise. I think..." She paused, remembering back to the way a few of them had looked at Tim. "I think some realized he was trying to take things in a direction I didn't like. One guy even suggested I have a talk with my husband, make sure we had clear-cut rules. We never got around to it. We had a fabulous fight that night. A few days later, I found the lump. And that's all she wrote."

Absently, she twisted the ring on her finger. *Remade...* She'd remade herself. Scarred, stronger. And better, she realized. The woman she was wouldn't have even bothered going to that club with Tim. The woman she was *now* wouldn't have bothered with *Tim.*

"I don't tend to do the club scene," he said, his voice cutting into the silence.

Staring at his bowed head as he continued to play, Chaili said, "I can't say that bothers me. But if you don't do the club scene, how do you know about Blue's?"

"Well..." He slanted a look up at her. "If you're looking to find a certain sort of...partner, discreetly, Blue's got the right place for you." Shrugging, he said, "It's not what I'd prefer but it does the job. Some of the people who use the club... Well, it's everything. They live it, breathe it. It's their life. Not just in the bedroom, but everywhere. If that's what works for you, then that's fine. I've found what works for me. I'm not living any sort of lifestyle but my own. Trying to fit into somebody else's version of a lifestyle interests me about as much as what my neighbors had for dinner last night."

The knot that had been tightening in her gut started to ease a little. "So what did they have for dinner?"

He shot her a wide grin. "What the fuck...ah, what the hell do I care?" Shifting his attention back to the piano, he said, "I tend to want to be in control in the bedroom. That's just who I am. I'm bossy, I'm pushy and I don't plan on changing who I am. It wouldn't work anyway."

"I don't want to change you." She settled back down on the bench and leaned against him for a moment.

The music stilled for a moment. "I know that. I'm kind of amazed by it. But I know." The music resumed. "There are things that I find...useful from the lifestyle that I use. Safe words. Makes it easier, especially when I don't know limits. Then there's the fun stuff..."

"Fun stuff?"

"Hmmm. What are your limits, Chaili? What don't you like?"

"Ah..." She licked her lips. Her heart bumped against her ribs and she could feel the slow crawl of blood creeping up her neck, staining her face red. Tugging at the neckline of her shirt, she squirmed around on the seat, trying to figure what to say, how much to say. If she even knew *what* to say...

This was a lot harder than she would have thought. A more

personal discussion, she'd never had. "I'm not into group stuff. No threesomes, foursomes, moresomes."

"Moresomes?" He paused for a minute and started to laugh. "Nah. Don't worry. Moresomes aren't an issue and I'll beat the shit out of the man who even suggests it. Just you and me, Chaili. As long as we're together, it's just you, just me. I won't have another woman, you won't have another man."

"What if I want another woman?" she asked teasingly, although that was something else that had been pushed at her.

"Don't." He shot her a look. "If you decide you want somebody else, anybody else, let me know and we end it. I don't share, Chaili. At all."

"I don't either." She held his gaze, watched as the hot, pleased little smile curled his lips before he went back to playing, like his entire life was wrapped up in that piano. She understood, though. Marc's mind just functioned better when he played. He'd always been like that. He'd even studied better when he played the piano. If he could find a way to cook and play the piano, he'd do it. Bathe. Shop. Sleep. Everything.

"So there's that ground rule established. The watching thing..." He shrugged. "If you get the need to watch we can always head over to Blue's. I don't much mind that. You can wear a skirt, even. I'll yank it up and show you things that pussy you married couldn't even begin to think of."

She laughed, the sound more than a little breathless. More than a little nervous. "Okay."

"I don't want to share you in any way, though. That includes letting another man see you when I fuck you. Do you need that?"

"No..." The word was barely a whisper.

"Good." He stopped playing, turned on the bench to stare at her. "What do you need?"

You. Just *you*...but she didn't dare tell him that. "I don't *need* any of it. I just..."

"No hiding," he rasped, shaking his head. "I don't want you hiding. I'll tell you what I want, what I need, but I want the same from you."

"You strip me bare, you know that?" Looking away, she stared out the window at the endless expanse of the water. "What we've done gives me what I need. I can take it harder, rougher...I like it harder sometimes. I want that. Other times, I just want..." She shrugged, reaching up to toy with the neckline of her shirt.

"I just want a man to make love to me. Just us. I won't ever be any man's slave, though, and it all stops at the bedroom door... Sexually, I'm more inclined to submit, but I don't think you can call me a submissive because I'm not *looking* just to please you. That's not my primary concern. It's a big thought in my head, but..." She shrugged and closed her eyes. "I want something out of it too. Maybe that sounds selfish, but..."

"That's not selfish. It's human. I sure as hell want something out of sex, even if I want to make sure you come so hard you're still feeling me inside you an hour later." He wrapped his arm around her upper body, pulling her back against him. "I think we've already established we're not talking about any sort of typical D/s relationship, baby girl. Let's worry about what *we* need, not what rules others live by."

He slipped his hand under her shirt, his fingertips tracing over the tattoo. "What else do you need? What do you like?"

"It's your turn now," she said, her voice shaky.

"Hmmm." Marc turned his face into her hair, brought his other hand around her and pressed it to her belly, fingers spread wide. "If it's sex, I'll want to control it for the most part. That's just me. Like if I tell you I want you to strip naked and

161

eat dinner that way so I can stare at you and think about the many different ways I'm going to fuck you, I'd want you to do it."

"And if I say no, because I'd be cold, then what?"

"I'd turn up the heat. But if it really bothered you..." He shrugged. "Then maybe we'd just come back to the issue in a few weeks. And I wouldn't drop it unless you gave me a good reason. Your scars aren't a reason. They're part of you and I find you beautiful."

Tears clogged her throat. "I don't see how."

"Take off your shirt."

With a watery laugh, she whispered, "Is this a sex thing?"

His hands gripped her shirt. "It's a 'Marc worships you and wants you to see what he sees' thing," he whispered, dragging the material up.

She let him. When he turned her around, he traced his fingers over the scar. "This doesn't make you any less, Chaili," he whispered. "You're still the same funny, amazing, smart woman I've known most of my life. Do you still do the work down at the kid's center in the summer?"

"Yes." She tucked her chin, unable to look at him. But watching his hands on her flesh was...

Well. Startlingly erotic.

"And when Shera gets sick with her asthma, are you the one who's nagging her about her medicine, going to the doctor, all that stuff?"

"Yes."

"And you're the one who nagged her into quitting smoking, aren't you?"

She grimaced. "Hell. It wasn't that hard. When you're sitting there dog sick from the drugs, recovering from surgery, and you tell your friend you'd like her to not end up dealing with cancer...well. She got the point."

"Not everybody would care enough to try." He nuzzled her neck and then went to his knees, tracing his fingers along the tattoo. Pressing his lips to it, along the curves of the butterfly's wings. Then shifting his attention to the scars. "This didn't change who you are."

Tears pricked at her eyes as he tugged the shirt back on. "And I find that tattoo hella sexy, by the way."

A startled laugh escaped her and she rolled her eyes. "Whatever."

He turned her back around, resting his chin on her shoulder as they stared out over the water. "I want to control sex. I won't always need it, but for the most part, I'll want to. I've already had about ten thousand different fantasies about the ways I want to tie you up, tie you down..." He cupped her in his hand and pressed the heel of his palm against her mound. "I plan on doing the first one tonight."

"You've already tied me up." Breath hitched in her lungs, just thinking about it.

"Spur of the moment. This is something I've been thinking about...for days." Lightly, he rubbed the heel of his hand against her.

Her eyes fluttered closed and she sagged in his embrace, clutching at him for balance. "I'm fine with being bound."

"Good. I already know you like being spanked. Does it need to be more?"

She grimaced. "No. I...I don't mind certain sorts of floggers, but if it's something that leaves marks or really hurts, I don't much care for it."

"I don't plan on doing anything that leaves a mark. And

pain doesn't do anything for me. I'm a control freak, but that's it." He continued to stroke her through her skirt. "Do you want me to make you come?"

"Yes..."

"Pull it up."

She went to reach for the tie, but he said, "Up...not off. I like seeing my hands on you while you're naked under that pretty skirt. My fingers inside your pussy."

Shuddering, she gathered the skirt in her hands and dragged it up, holding the panel in one hand, and gripped his arm for balance as he started to stroke her. "Your turn now," he whispered into her ear.

"I hate being made to beg."

"Hmmm...well, sometimes I'll do that. But you know how to make me stop." He plunged two fingers inside her sex, twisted them. Withdrew. Over and over. "Have you ever been hogtied?"

"Nuh...no." Oh, hell. She couldn't have this conversation while he was touching her like this. Finger-fucking her and expecting her to talk... Closing her eyes, she focused on his touch, clenching down around him as he stroked, teased, tormented.

She felt his chest rumbling against her back and she groaned. "What?"

"You're not listening," he teased, pulling his hand out and swatting her lightly.

She gasped at the stinging contact against her sex.

"What about that?" he rasped. "We didn't discuss that. Is this allowed?"

She couldn't...oh, shit. Sucking in a desperate breath of air, she whispered, "Do it again."

He spanked her pussy again, lightly, the stinging contact

with her clit sparking through her like fire. "I guess this is allowed..." He started to finger fuck her again.

"Do it again," she demanded.

"No."

"Damn it, Marc. Do it again..."

Suddenly, he wasn't touching her.

Staggering, she slammed a hand against the bench to catch her balance as he moved away. "A few more things, Chaili," Marc rasped.

"Marc," she groaned, her head spinning, her body aching. Turning around, she glared at him.

"Sorry, baby girl." His voice was wry, rough. "You make me lose my head. That control thing... I'm serious about it and when you push certain buttons, it makes me want to do things like flip you over my knee and paddle your ass."

She blinked, the image dancing through her mind. *Oh*... She bit her lower lip to keep from whimpering.

"You okay with that?"

She swallowed. "Do you know when to let up?" she asked warily.

"Yes. And if you want me to stop, you know how to make me."

She blinked, nodded. She rose to go to him. "Have we gotten these rules established well enough, Marc?"

Marc felt the threads of his control straining to the breaking point. He caught her back against him. "I can't bend you over my knee if you're standing," he purred against her ear. He guided her over to the piano, sat with his back to the instrument, guiding her so she lay facedown over his knees. Stroking his hand along her rump, he squeezed lightly. She shuddered. "I'm going to give you my cock when I'm done. I want to watch you take it in your mouth," he said.

She groaned.

He brought his hand down, watched as her pretty, ivory flesh went pink. He did it again. She shuddered and cried out. Again. Again. He reached down, stroked her clit, teasing the erect little bud lightly and feeling her quiver. Then he spanked her again, a little harder. Then a little harder. Every few swats, he'd go back to tease her clitoris. Then, as he went to bring his hand down on her ass, she cried out and came.

Her body twisted over his knee and he stroked a hand down her back, pleasure streaking through him. Delight. Need.

Mine...

Chapter Eleven

The oven timer buzzed before they got to finish.

Chaili was actually pretty okay with that.

She needed a few minutes to recover.

He'd spanked her to climax.

Seated at the island, sipping a Diet Coke and watching while Marc cut up a salad, she tried to catch her breath and wrap her mind around that simple fact. He'd *spanked* her to climax. Desperate to get them back to someplace that felt comfortable, she said lightly, "You're surprisingly domestic, Marc."

"I told you, if I wanted anything other than carryout or mac and cheese." He shrugged. Then he gave her a telling look. "I love the way you say my name when you're in the middle of an orgasm."

Her throat went dry and she gulped down half of her drink. She tried to get back on level footing and look what happened...

"You keep trying to put up a wall. What's the deal with that?"

She reached over and plucked an olive out of the bowl. "No walls. What do you mean?"

"Chaili."

Shit. Closing her eyes, she lowered her head. How did she respond to that, she wondered. *I've loved you my entire life...and I don't know if this is going to last...*

"If you're already having doubts about us, we're doomed,

you know," he said quietly.

"I don't even think there is an *us* yet, Marc."

She looked up as he reached for the towel lying on the counter by them and slowly wiped his hands off.

"There's been an *us* for a lot longer than I realized," he said softly. "It just took me a little while to see it."

She turned away, looking for anything to stare at, to occupy her mind. "Marc, for there to be an *us*, we'd need to know."

"Do you know what I've missed the past few years? More than anything I can think of?" He stared at her, his eyes lingering over her face, studying it. Searching it. "You. I'd find myself thinking about you. And I'd call you. Sometimes you were there. Sometimes you weren't. When you weren't...it made the day darker. When you were, it...well...you made the day. There was an us. I just didn't see it. Come on. Let's eat."

Every time, damn it. Every time she was almost close to level, he shattered the very foundation under her feet. Sliding off the stool, she edged around the island, keeping a little bit of distance between them. "Could we eat outside?" she asked, glancing toward the doorway that led to the deck she'd seen. There was no real desire to sit outside, but if she had a few more minutes...

The look in Marc's eyes told her he knew exactly what she was doing. But he shrugged and gestured. "Sure. Take the basket of bread and our drinks. I'll be out with the rest in a minute."

She looked at the island with the salad, the dish of lasagna. "I can carry things out."

"So can I," he said mildly. "Go out outside. There's a fire pit on the table. It's gas. Why don't you light it?"

"Okay."

Damn it. She'd wanted a few minutes to try and get herself under control and now she was going to be eating a dinner by firelight with him...

Every damn way I turn...

Outside, she set the glasses together at one end. She'd thought about setting them farther apart—him at the head, her at the foot of the table. Just to give herself some of that badly needed space. And yeah, that would have gone over really well. So instead she did what just felt natural, the two of them, sitting side by side, staring out over the water.

Jerking his chain wouldn't be smart.

Although it would be a hell of a lot easier if he'd give her a little bit of space. Just a little.

She fiddled with the knobs on the fire pit and watched as it flared to life, smiling absently. It was pretty—brightly colored rocks that looked like glass in the base, reflecting the light. Easing back, she turned away and moved to stand at the railing, staring out over the lake. The wind kicked up, blowing her hair and tangling her skirt around her legs.

Hearing the door open, she turned around and saw him balancing the plates, waiter style on his arm. She laughed and leaned back against the railing. "I forgot you used to do that sort of thing for a living," she said.

"A handy skill, juggling four plates," he said dryly. He set them down and headed back inside. "Back in a minute."

A few minutes later, he was back outside with silverware and cloth napkins in a deep shade of burgundy. She sat down, about ready to pop off with another quip, but she glanced up, saw him watching her. Waiting. She needed to stop this, she knew. Blowing out a breath, she said, "It looks pretty decent for a guy who used to burn mac and cheese."

"Yeah, well, wait until you try it, smart ass," he muttered.

She smiled and took a bite of the salad. It was good, although salads were easy.

"You afraid to try the lasagna?"

Rolling her eyes, she scooped up a bite and tried it. Then she blinked and shot him a look. "Wow."

A smug grin curved his lips as he cut into his. "Told you."

"You really need to work on that humility problem of yours, Marc. People just don't know what to make of overly humble people."

He chuckled and for a few minutes they ate in a light, companionable silence.

The lasagna was probably better than any she could make. Of course, she didn't do much cooking lately. Sometimes she and Shera decided to do something, but for the most part, she stuck with the cheap and the basic, out of necessity. "Who taught you to cook?" she asked after she'd done everything but lick the enamel off the plate. Breaking a piece of her bread off, she told herself she wasn't going to be jealous when he said it had been a girlfriend.

"My drummer's wife." He leaned back, eyeing her like he knew what she was thinking. "She's my assistant. You've met her. Ilona?"

"Yeah." Cute. Funny. Biting sense of humor. Chaili had liked her. "I'm surprised she had the patience to do it."

"Oh, she's got the patience of a saint. She just hides it well." He glanced at her plate. "Want more? I made enough to feed an army."

"No." She patted her belly. "I ate far more than I needed to anyway."

She nipped another bite of the bread and immediately

choked when he said, "Take your shirt off."

Reaching for her glass of water, she glared at him. "Are you trying to kill me?"

"Absolutely not." He smiled at her, stroking his thumb down the line of his jaw. "Take off your shirt."

She looked around, but the way the layout of his house was designed, nobody would be able to see them unless they were either *on* the deck with them, or out on the water.

Still, she was blushing as she stripped the shirt off. Folding it, she set it down on the table and lifted her head to find him skimming his eyes along her body. They didn't even hesitate on the scars, she noticed. It was like the scars were the same to him as her belly, her legs... Except they weren't. Closing her eyes, she fought the urge to hide, could even feel her shoulders slumping, her feet itching with the need to turn away.

"Look at me."

Staring at him through her lashes, she held her hands fisted at her sides.

"You ready for dessert?"

The look on her face might have been comical, except there was nothing funny about the way she kept trying to pull away from him. He was tired of it. It was like she couldn't stop herself, and even though she wasn't backpedaling as much now as she had been, he figured the best thing to do was just keep her off balance a little.

Seemed fair.

He'd been off balance ever since he'd walked into *Escortè* and seen her standing there.

"Dessert?" she echoed, looking down at her bare chest and then up at him. Sighing, she brushed her hair back and rested her elbows on the table. "You really plan to make me eat dessert naked, Marc?"

"You're not naked," he pointed out. Echoing her pose, he held her gaze even though all he wanted to do was shove the table out of the way—would be kind of hard to do that too. The table had been built into the deck. That little fact didn't matter. He still wanted to do it, wanted to lay her out on the long bench, spread her thighs, hold her open and bare and strip away all the barriers, all the walls... and just have her.

Have all of her. Have everything.

No walls. No barriers.

Just them.

She smirked at him. "Okay, so I'm wearing a skirt. Close enough to naked. What's the point of this?"

"The point is, I want to see you sitting there, naked under that skirt. Firelight on your skin. And I want to think about what I'm going to do to you next," he said. "I'll be back in a few minutes."

He left her sitting there, face flushed, lips parted. And for a minute, he thought maybe she'd be too distracted to think about how uncomfortable she was.

He dumped the dishes in the sink. It was Sunday—that meant tomorrow Heloise would be in to clean. Thank God. Normally, he'd at least try to make a dent in the mess he'd made. His mom had drilled that into his head, but he didn't want to think about anything other than Chaili at this point.

He grabbed the dessert from the fridge, just a single plate. He hadn't made this. Dessert, he couldn't do. He either rushed it or forgot and burned things, or something and they never turned out right.

But he knew a lady who made a mean chocolate mousse...

Ilona was going to kill him if he kept begging for favors. He just might owe her a kidney or something if this kept up.

Back out on the deck, he saw Chaili sitting there, fidgeting with the fringe on her skirt with one hand, the other gripping her shoulder, partially hiding her chest.

She lifted her head and for a moment, he just stared.

How in the hell had he missed this? Standing there, looking in those jewel-toned eyes, watching him in that way she had, how that slow smile tugged at her lips, feeling that kick to his gut...how had he missed this?

Clearing his throat, he headed over to the table and sat next to her, straddling the bench. He lifted her knees, drawing her into the cradle of his body. "You know, when I was headed over to *Escortè*, the night of that party...I started thinking," he said, taking a spoon and dipping it into the mousse.

"Thinking, huh?" She leaned in, peering at the bowl. "Oh, damn. Is that chocolate?"

"Yep. And if you're going to be a smart ass, I'll keep it for myself." He took the bite he'd been planning on giving to her and slid it into his mouth, winking at her. "I can speak from experience...it's delicious."

She narrowed her eyes. "You shouldn't tempt a woman about chocolate, Marc. It's not fair."

"You shouldn't keep poking at me, unless you really want a reaction," he said, shrugging. "Anyway, I was heading over there, irritated as hell that I was going to have to put up with some woman I didn't know. Most of the women Shera has at *Escortè* are nice ladies, I know that. Polite, they can talk about shit that's *way* over my head, but..." He shrugged. "They bore me."

"Then why do it?" She made a grab for the spoon.

He caught her wrist. "Nope. I feed you."

Sighing, she snuggled in against him.

"Open." He scooped up a bite, held it up.

She took it, closed her lips and moaned.

The sound of it shot straight to his dick. Damn it. He fed her another bite and this time, she made a little humming sound under her breath. "Gimme more," she demanded.

"Be patient."

He ate some more, grinning at her as she shot him a look that threatened to send him to the hospital. "You've got a thing for chocolate, I see."

"Yes, I do." She poked him in the ribs. "You're bordering into mean territory there, pal."

"Yeah, yeah." He fed her a few more bites, relishing the way she relaxed against him, the way she smiled. Yeah, he was really questioning just how he'd missed this.

"You never answered me," she said quietly.

"Answered...oh. *Escortè*...you're distracting me again, you know. You keep making these little humming sounds while you're eating and it's like you're getting turned on just by the chocolate, and my dick's getting jealous." He helped himself to another bite and then fed her one. "It's easy. She's careful about who she hires and the women like the money, they like the job...most of them know she's going to unleash holy hell if they violate the agreements they sign so I know it's...safe. For the most part. Usually there's one girl she sets me up with and I like her well enough." He shrugged. "I guess she was busy that night. Thank God."

"But why do it? I mean, hell, Marc...you can't tell me you've got trouble finding dates," she said, tipping her head back and staring up at him.

"It's not the finding them," he muttered. Dropping the spoon into the bowl, he eased her off his lap and turned around, staring out over the water. "It's keeping things on a level I'm comfortable, without doing something or saying something that will piss somebody off. There was a woman I was just keeping a friendly thing with— Ah..." He slanted a look at her and shrugged. "This is complicated...but there were just a mess of screwed-up relationships. The worst one was a few years ago. A friend... Ah. Well. We'd been friends. It got to be more. Then it wasn't. Things didn't go well from there."

Chaili lifted the spoon, scooping more of the mousse into her mouth. Then, she held a bite to his lips. "Ended bad, huh?"

Blowing out a breath, he said quietly, "It was my manager. Lily. We'd been going along fine, then she up and messes around with a friend of mine. I walked in. Then I walked out and packed up her shit, told her to get out. They told me I'm taking it too personally. Whatever. That lasted about a week and then one day, she comes out here, wants to talk. First she tried just..." He paused, twisting it over in his mind.

Chaili snorted. "She thought she could screw you into letting it go?"

"That sums it up. I didn't buy it. Told her to leave. Then she tried convincing me how it was a horrible mistake and she was so sorry. When that didn't work..." He closed his eyes, blew out a breath. This was it. The thing that sent him spinning around the country, the world, for months on end. Rarely stopping for more than five minutes. "She told me if I tried to walk away, she was going to tell everybody I raped her. That I abused her. She tried to claim there was video..." He trailed off, waiting for that punch of anger, that twist of shame.

All that was there, though, was some bit of resignation. He'd really cared about Lily.

Really.

It wouldn't have ever been love, he knew that. But she'd mattered to him. And then she'd done that.

"She would hurt you that way," Chaili said, her voice all but vibrating with fury.

He shrugged jerkily. "Hey, up until a week or so ago, I was just having some seriously fucked-up luck when it came to women. Maybe it's because I was seeing the wrong ones."

He went to touch her shoulder, but she brushed his hand away, surging up off the bench to pace.

Well, he mused, she wasn't too concerned about her lack of clothes now. Her short, deep brown hair was mussed and it got worse as she shoved her hands through it. "How in the hell could she even *say* something like that? Was she fucked up in the head or what?"

"Well, yeah." When she turned to look at him, Marc shrugged. "Good a reason as any."

He caught her hand and tugged her over to him, down onto his lap. "Calm down." He stroked a hand up her back, her shoulders, cupping his hand over her neck. "It's over and done."

"Don't tell me to calm down." She glared at him, a snarl twisting her lips. "That kind of shit is just plain evil. What made her stop?"

He studied her face, heaving out a breath. Figured he might as well go ahead and finish it. "My sister," he said, jerking a shoulder in a shrug. "She...well, we were at my place. Supposed to go out to dinner. The two of them showed up at the same time and I ended up in the studio with Lily while Shera was upstairs. I wasn't kidding when I said she was fucked up in the head. Lily had been using for a while. It was getting out of hand. I dunno, something set Shera's mental alarm off. I've got the studio set up to record if I want. Shera's done it a few times...when I'm just messing around, working on a new piece. She slipped in. I didn't even notice. I was trying to pretend nobody was there and I just wanted Lily to *leave*.

"Lily was high, hell, I ended up having to call a car for her, she was so strung out. So when she started with the threats, Shera had it all on video. Lily was getting all ugly and I ignored her for the most part, even though I guess part of me was worried. I told her to she had to go and she was heading to the door, swearing and making threats when Shera stopped us in the hall. She made us both go into the living room and she popped the DVD into the recorder. Shera told Lily if she ever bothered me again, that DVD would hit the inbox of every musician she could find—nobody wants to work with a manager who is going to pull that kind of shit. Lily came after Shera, but..."

Chaili grinned, a mean, happy little smile. "She hit her, didn't she? Hard?"

Marc shook his head. "I'm surrounded by bloodthirsty women. Yeah. Popped her one. Lily went down cold. That night..." He looked away. "She overdosed that night. Ended up in the hospital. She finally got clean, though. I heard from her a few months ago. She sent me a letter, told me she was sorry, wanted to...make amends."

"Did you tell her to fuck off?"

"You swear too much, Chaili," he teased. Resting a hand on her breastbone, he held her gaze. "I called her. She wanted to meet for dinner. Talk old times. Apologize. I told her she could apologize well enough over the phone if she had to, but it wasn't necessary." At the time, he'd been too angry with her, still. Now he realized it didn't matter anymore. He didn't need to be angry about it, but he also didn't need to see her again.

"Like hell," she snapped.

He shook his head. "If she needs to do it, she needs to do it. I'm not angry with her. I just figured that out too. There's no reason for me to be. She was strung out on drugs half the time, on sex the other half. She maintained a good front and I didn't even realize how bad off she was..." Frowning, he shrugged. "I wasn't good for her. If I'd seen how screwed up she was, maybe—*hey!*"

He rubbed his chest, glaring at her. "You trying to poke a hole in me or what?"

"Don't make excuses for her." She wiggled off his lap, shooting him a dark look. "That pisses me off. I can't stand it when people make excuses for addicts."

"Shit." He closed his eyes and rubbed his hands over his face.

Chaili's mom had done more than a little time in and out of treatment centers. Her drug of choice had been alcohol, though. When Chaili was a sophomore in college, her mom had been riding home with a boyfriend and they'd been in an accident— alcohol had been involved on both sides. Nobody survived. Neither of the drivers had been sober, but since Chaili's mom was the passenger, insurance had been forced to pay Chaili the full benefits and it had let her finish college.

But it left her with little tolerance for addicts. Considering some of the shit he'd seen her deal with most of her life, he could understand.

"I'm not making excuses, exactly," he said quietly. "But if you're involved with somebody, you should see when they need help."

"And she could have told you she needed it, instead of trying to cry rape when you wanted out of a relationship that wasn't working," Chaili said, her voice cool.

It was a little more complicated than that, but...hell. How

had they gotten around to discussing this anyway?

"You know, we have this way of straying off topic," he said, crooking a grin at her. "I have plans to do all sorts of dirty, unspeakable acts to you. And you keep talking."

She rolled her eyes. "You don't seem to have problems speaking the unspeakable."

"True." He caught her skirt in his hand, tugged her to him. "I plan on tying you up and fucking you shortly. Want to hear how I'm going to do it?"

Her breath caught. He loved the way it did that...a little hitch in her chest, like he'd just sucked the oxygen right out of her lungs. He loved it. She bit her lip and then shrugged, glancing past him to the bowl of mousse. "There's still chocolate left."

"Maybe we could take it with us. I wouldn't mind seeing you spread it all over me and licking it off," he teased.

She made a face at him. "No. I have issues with...um. Food and sex. They don't go together." She sank back down onto his lap and picked up the spoon. "Besides, I don't want to miss a single bite of it."

"Issues with food and sex, huh?"

"Yes. It's unsanitary." She wrinkled her nose, scooping a bite of mousse and offering it to him.

He shook his head, resting his hands on her hips. "Okay. I'll keep that in mind...a weird thing to have limits on, but no food and sex."

"Hey, sanitary issues aren't weird," she said, nudging him with her finger. "It's just like having good body hygiene after...well..."

She trailed off and he watched as a blush crept over her cheeks. "Body hygiene is important. Showers and stuff after the, ah...anal sex."

"Absolutely." Fuck, she was so damned cute. So damned beautiful.

"You're snickering at me," she said, heaving out a sigh.

"I'm not."

"You are." She squirmed around on his lap.

The uncomfortable look on her face had him realizing this wasn't just a random thought firing off in her head, and something started to burn low in his gut. "If you say the *T* word, I'm going to get pissed," he said mildly. "I can connect the dots well enough and I see the picture."

One reason he didn't mesh very well in a hardcore D/s scene was because of some of the asses he'd met. He'd encountered a few jerks, like Tim, who thought it was cool to use humiliation to 'teach a sub'. And he already had a feeling he knew where this was going.

"Tim did everything from trying to push threesomes on me to buying a cane—which he *never* used—and then he started trying to cross harder lines. Said I needed 'learn my place' and once he tried to make me go down on him after anal. It's disgusting." She threw her spoon down. "He wanted a happy little sub but that was never what I wanted. He wanted me in the place he'd assigned for me and he couldn't see that wasn't a place *I* wanted."

Sliding his hand up her back, he sank his fingers into the tight muscles of her neck, massaging them. "You only belong in the place where you want to be. And I kind of like the place you made for yourself. I don't want you anywhere else."

"Good." She tilted her head and smiled at him. "You know...you were supposed to be telling me all these dirty, unspeakable things."

"Oh. Yes." Closing his eyes, he continued to massage her neck. He needed to get focused and stop thinking about how he wanted to pound that asshole ex of hers bloody. "We'll get to those. As soon as you're done with your dessert."

"I'm done now."

Chapter Twelve

Chaili stared at her reflection in the mirror over the couch.

She'd expected him to take her to his bedroom but he hadn't.

They were in the living room. Or she guessed he called it his living room, although the massive sprawl of the room put her piddly little living room to shame. The couch was a long, liquid spread of gleaming leather and she was standing in front of it, her back to Marc as he bound her.

Thanks to the mirror in front of her, she was able to watch the entire thing too.

He didn't use rope or cuffs.

Bondage tape was a new experience. It had more give than the leather restraints she was used to, but considering the time Marc was taking as he bound her arms behind her back, crossed with her forearms pressed together, she didn't know if it mattered that there was a little bit of give in the tape.

When he finished with her arms, he dropped the tape down onto the couch and stood there, his hands on her hips, staring at their reflection in the mirror. "You're beautiful," he said gruffly.

Chaili swallowed.

He reached around, tugging at the tie that held her skirt up. It fell away, leaving her naked before him. Then he trailed his fingers up, tracing around the edges of her tattoo, along the delicates lines of the butterfly, stroking the scars. Her lids drifted low, shielding her eyes.

"Look at me. I want to see you, watching me as I watch you...you're so damned amazing," he whispered. Abruptly, he stopped. "I want a picture of you. Is that off limits?"

Chaili blinked. "Ah... a picture?"

"Yes. You. With me."

She looked down at her scarred chest and then back up, into his intense golden eyes. Unsteadily, she said, "Okay."

He was gone before she could say another word and she squeezed her eyes closed, refusing to think about it. Pictures...shit. She wasn't going to let herself get self-conscious. She'd think about the way the tape felt...the way it felt as he stared at her. And what he might be planning. Her breath caught in her chest, as she eyed the tape. Was he done?

He'd said something about hog tying...

"Change your mind?"

She looked up and saw him in the doorway, holding a camera. A tripod.

"Nuh...no," she stammered. She didn't think, at least. "I mean, it's just for you."

Something flashed in his eyes and the smile that curved his lips was almost wild. "Damn straight. Just for me." He set the camera up, angling it a little. He glanced up at her, had her shift around a little. Then he moved to stand behind her, bringing one arm around her. "I should have thought of this before I tied you," he said gruffly. "I'll do more...but for now..."

He spread his hand open over the tattoo. There was something oddly possessive, protective, gentle about the way he touched her. Chaili closed her eyes, lowered her head, struggling to catch her breath.

She heard a low, electronic whine and opened her eyes,

saw something in Marc's hand. A remote, she realized. He had a remote for the camera. Jerking her head up, she stared at him in shock and he took another. "Look at me," he said.

She did and he covered her mouth with his, a soft, gentle kiss.

Another picture.

Then the gentleness fell away and the hand he'd splayed over the tattoo lifted, cupping her cheek as he thrust his tongue inside her mouth, deep. Hard. Over and over. It was a deep, brutal possession and she wasn't even aware of the camera taking picture after picture.

He undid her. Stripped her bare. Shaking and gasping for breath by the time he lifted his head, Chaili swayed, caught off balance. His hands at her hips steadied her. "Stay there," he rasped.

Like I can do anything else, she thought, dazed. Licking her lips, she tried to will some strength into her shaking legs, but it wasn't happening.

In the mirror, she caught sight of herself and her breath hitched once more in her throat.

Her face was flushed.

Her eyes glowed.

With her arms bound behind her, the flat plane of her chest seemed almost vulnerable...and the tattoo, the marks of her scars almost surreal. For the first time, she realized they weren't quite as disfiguring as she'd always thought. No. It wasn't what she would have wanted, but as much as she'd been telling herself she'd accepted herself, she hadn't fully managed it.

Yet.

But maybe she was getting closer.

Marc nudged her over a little and she blinked, feeling more than a little off balance, although it had nothing to do with what was going on in the physical world. Everything to do with what was happening inside her head.

Licking her lips, she looked down at the couch. She hadn't quite processed what she was seeing before Marc nudged her back into place. "Bend over," he whispered in her ear.

Oh. Hell.

Chaili bent over the round black leather ottoman he'd moved onto the couch, biting her lip as she waited for it to shift under her weight. It didn't. He nudged her up higher and then, with his eyes intent on hers, he reached down, caught her lower leg, bringing it higher.

"Okay?" he asked softly as he brought her ankle almost flush with her thigh.

Chaili groaned.

"Is that a yes or a no?"

"Yes..." He was going to tie her. Like this. Pressing her face against the leather, she closed her eyes, sucked in a desperate breath. There was a bit of pull in her muscles, but not much. She was active, flexible as hell, a fact Marc obviously seemed to appreciate.

A fact he was appreciating *slowly*.

Shuddering, she fisted her hands, the one part of her she could easily move, and sank her nails into her palms, while the need and hunger sank its claws into her belly.

Finally, he finished. He'd hogtied her, but modified it—her ankles were bound to her thighs and her hands were bound behind her back, forearm to forearm. The position left her unable to move, and she felt completely exposed.

"I told you I wanted to see you bound," he teased, pushing

her hair back and peering into her eyes. "Can you move much?"

She tried, squirming around; she could move her hands. That was about it. Lying as she was, it wasn't even that easy to move her head. She felt completely helpless. It was erotic as hell. Frustrating as hell.

Giving him the power...the trust to do this.

The real twist was that she trusted him a hell of a lot more than she would have trusted Tim. He'd always tried to take things too far.

"Okay. You got to see it. You going to do those dirty, unspeakable things to me now?" she asked, swallowing the knot that settled in her throat, trying to forget those dark, unwelcome thoughts that tried to creep in.

He pressed a thumb between her eyebrows. "You know...I can tell when you start thinking about him. You get this line...right here." He stood, moved behind her. "It pisses me off, Chaili. You need to stop it."

The first spank, hard, almost too hard, caught her by surprise. She gasped and twisted. Perched on the leather ottoman, in what felt like a damned precarious position, she jolted hard enough that she might have fallen if he hadn't been there to steady her.

"Be still," he growled. "You think about him when I'm with you. Stop it."

He didn't do it again, moving to stand behind her.

She opened her mouth to snarl at him and then she groaned as he pushed her thighs apart and then sank deep inside her. No preparation.

No teasing. Just that deep, sudden penetration.

He took her rough, and fast, and the first orgasm caught her by surprise. While she was still gasping, he pulled away and she craned her head. Through the sweaty strands of her hair, she saw him. He was stripping his clothes away, watching her with burning eyes. "You going to think about him again while I'm with you like this?" he rasped.

Chaili closed her eyes. "Shit, Marc. I'm sorry, okay? I...he..."

He tangled his fingers in her hair and tugged her head up, staring into her eyes. "He can't come into your head unless you let him in. Just don't open the door."

He continued to watch her, his gaze searching. Finally, after long seconds passed, he stood and moved away, out of her sight again.

Squeezing her eyes closed, she twisted her wrists, jerking at the bonds that held her trapped.

"It's not as easy as that to undo them," Marc said from somewhere off behind her. "It's going to take more than just jerking at the tape. Of course, if you want me to let you go, just say the word."

Chaili curled her lip. She wasn't about to do that. She just...

Muttering under her breath, she continued to jerk at the bonds until he came up behind her.

Then he touched her.

One finger.

Slicked with something unbelievably cool against her heated flesh. Teasing her clit. Just her clit. Tingles, cool at first, and then more intense, spread through her. She groaned and squirmed on the leather that supported her weight, jerking against the restraints harder, twisting against them almost desperately. "Marc," she whispered.

"Unspeakable...dirty...things," he said slowly. He spread

the cheeks of her ass and she trembled, held still as she waited.

But he did nothing.

"What are you doing, damn it?"

"Watching you go crazy." He reached down and stroked her clit, then traced her gate with the tip of his finger and that tingly sensation started to burn, spreading everywhere he touched. "There's this gel you can use on a woman's clitoris. Doesn't work on every woman, but if it's going to work, you'll feel it pretty fast. Are you feeling anything?"

The sob caught in her throat and she twisted her wrists again in the tape. "Damn it, Marc..."

"I'll take that as a yes."

Yes??? Yeah. It was a yes. She ached, throbbed—could feel the blood pulsating...oh... Trembling as he stroked down and pushed one finger inside her, twisted his wrist.

She shrieked and clenched down around him, stunned by the intensity of the sensation.

A second time. A third time.

Each touch, each stroke was a cross between pleasure and the purest edge of pain.

And then he stopped, right when she was on the edge of climaxing.

She was trembling.

Marc stared at her as he grabbed the tube of lubricant from the couch. "That's one unspeakably dirty thing," he said, his voice raw, staring at her raised ass. "I've got you bound and restrained, so fucking turned on you're almost ready to beg me, aren't you?"

Her voice was a rough rasp as she demanded, "Is that what you want?"

"No. If it was, I'd tell you." He grabbed a small tube from the couch, took off the top and sprayed it on the narrow opening of her ass, watched as she flinched a little. As the spray went to work, he reached for the lubricant and opened it, slicking it over his cock, and squeezing more of it into his hand. "Now I'm going to fuck your ass."

She tensed.

"Is that a problem?"

"Marc...I..."

She jerked against the restraints—arms bound at her back, her ankles drawn up, tied to her thighs. He smoothed his free hand down her hip and then nudged her legs farther apart before he pressed his slickened fingers against her, preparing her. In. Out. The tight ring of muscles at her entrance resisted for a moment, then yielded, letting him know the relaxing spray was working. As he pushed past that first initial resistance, he closed his eyes, bit back a groan at how silken she was around him. "Is it a problem?" he asked again.

But all she did was moan, even as she tried to twist away. He held her steady with his free hand at her hip.

In. Out. Preparing her. The low sound of her whimpering, the broken sound of her breathing, the trembling of her body, he noted every nuance of her reaction and once he had her ready, he moved between her bound thighs, using his hands to spread her open.

"You know how to make it stop, Chaili," he said gruffly. Tucking the head of his cock against the puckered mouth to her back entrance, he pressed against her. Slowly. Just the head...bit by slow, torturous bit, and oh, hell, it was amazing. "Now I'm doing another dirty, unspeakable thing...pushing into this hot, tight hole and you can't touch yourself. Does it drive you crazy, baby?"

"Yes, damn it!" She jerked again.

"Aw, now," he said gruffly, steadying her with a hand on the base of her spine. Stroking his fingers along her soft skin, he soothed her as he advanced another slow inch. "Be still now or you'll make me get all rough here. It's easier when you can touch yourself, isn't it?"

She panted, tried to pull away. Catching her hips, he held her steady, the blood pounding in his ears, hunger biting into him, threatening to tear him into shreds.

He eased back, giving her a minute, but she cried out, clenched down around him in protest. "You want more, baby girl?"

"Yes, damn it. Please, Marc?"

He pushed deeper, waited until he felt the resistance and then he stopped, pulling out, keeping at just at that depth, a slow, easy pace. "You didn't answer me. It's easier when you can touch yourself, bring yourself to orgasm that way while this happens, right?"

"Yes. It's easier..." A soft, pink flush spread all over her skin and she pushed back harder on him, taking him in deeper. It was pure bliss as she eased around him, moving with him. Splaying his fingers over the base of her spine, he started to ride her hard, feet spread out, head bowed, staring at her. Just her.

"I don't want to give you easy." He surged deep, held there as she tensed. Bending down over her, he murmured in her ear, "I want to give you what you need...I want to make you feel like nobody else ever has, like nobody else can...and I want to make it to where you can never build another fucking wall, where you can never think of another man when we're together."

A sob ripped from her. Propping his elbow next to her head, he waited as she shuddered, as she trembled and shook. "I won't give you easy," he promised again. "But I'll damn well give you everything I can."

He stood back up and started to do just that.

Deep, steady strokes.

She cried out with each one. Soft, broken little sobs.

"Come for me, baby girl," he rasped. "Come for me."

"I *can't*," she whimpered. "Not like this...not without..."

He slid a hand down, slid it around to press it against her belly. "Doesn't this feel good?" he asked, rolling his hips against her ass. "It feels damn fucking good to me. Your ass is hot, snug silk around my dick and you're so fucking pretty like this, bound for me, here just for me...doesn't it feel good, Chaili..." He bent down and pressed his lips to her shoulder. "Having to have me do hot, dirty, unspeakable things to you..."

She trembled and under his hand he felt the silken muscles of her belly clench. "You, bound, waiting and open... Your ass all but grabbing at me each time I sink my dick inside you... Doesn't it feel good?" He eased his hand down lower. Lower. Felt the muscles of her belly tense.

But before he reached her clit, her entire body quaked and she tightened around him, tighter...tighter... "Aw, fuck." He gritted his teeth as she clenched down around him and came with a broken, ragged cry.

And as she finally fell, he let go as well, hunkering over her and surging deep, echoing the hard, driving hunger that rode him every damn time he saw her.

He'd wipe those shadows from her eyes...somehow, damn it.

And she wouldn't keep thinking about anything, or anybody else, when she was with him.

Chapter Thirteen

She could hear the music drifting from his studio.

Bent over her laptop, Chaili let herself close her eyes for just a minute, let herself get lost in the music. If she wasn't careful, she was going to get lost in *him*.

"It's already happening, you twit," she muttered. *Already happened...* As the music for "True Believer" started to play, she groaned. No. It wasn't already happening. It had already *happened*. She'd been lost in Marc since they were teens, and before that? The infatuation had been well under way.

Pretending otherwise was just a waste of time.

She could remember sitting in the house with Shera, bent over homework, listening to him and a couple of the guys from his first band piecing together music. She'd been spending the night when he had first started composing "True Believer"—the strains of that song still made her shiver. It had been his breakout hit, the one that took him from being a fairly popular guy in the Chicago music scene to an international star.

She loved the song, but sometimes she also hated it. It marked the point when she started to lose him. Not that he'd ever really been hers, but at least she'd gotten to see him from time to time. She'd been able to console herself with that.

And it was before she'd made the biggest mistake of her life...

Asking him out that last time.

Having him smile at her. Pat on her shoulder like she was a

cute little puppy who'd amused him. *Nah. I'm beat... I just wanna crash for a while.* Then, the next day, she'd seen clips of him out at a party. When he'd been supposedly too tired to catch a movie. Yet he'd gone to a party with one of the shiny little perfect girls he always seemed to date.

A week later, she'd met Tim.

Six months after that, they were married.

Six months after that...

She rubbed a finger over the top edge of the tattoo, able to find it without even looking down.

How much different would her life have been if she hadn't married Tim? Jumping into that relationship certainly hadn't been the wisest decision she'd ever made. If she hadn't bothered with dating him? It wasn't like she hadn't already known what she liked, right? She'd maybe taken it a little darker, pushed her boundaries a little further. And yeah, she'd figured out just how far her limits were, but she'd learned a little more about pain, learned too much about rejection.

Life would have been just fine without all of that.

It might have made her stronger, but...

Marc's voice filled the house.

Deep. Strong. That raw, whiskey-soaked velvet. Wrapping around her, intoxicating her.

And she found herself being pulled back to the past night.

I want to make it to where you can never build another fucking wall, where you can never think of another man when we're together...

Why was she even wasting her time thinking about somebody who had hurt her so miserably bad?

Somebody who had thrown her out of his life when she'd needed help the most?

"Because I'm an idiot," she said sourly. "And I need to stop it."

Shoving it out of her head, she focused on the screen and even managed to tune Marc's voice out until it was just background noise. Mostly. Background noise that managed to send shivers up and down her spine.

She had a lot of work to get done and only so much time to do it. Twenty minutes back into work, she had to hit the Internet. She was thinking that what she wanted to do with Marc's website was just start from scratch and she had an idea for what she wanted, but she had yet to find *exactly* what she was looking for.

A hunt on the website she usually used was a waste of time. Yet again.

Closing her eyes, she rubbed her hands over her face, let herself pull up the idea she had in mind. Something different. The idiot who had screwed up her site design hadn't exactly had the wrong sort of *idea*, just bad execution, tacking it onto a design that wasn't right for it.

She could incorporate that sort of feel into the new design and already had an idea, but what kind of...

It hit her.

She went to her email and sketched out what she wanted to do, sent it to Marc. She didn't know who was handling this end now since he'd hired her himself, but she figured he'd handle forwarding it on. He'd have to run it by the rest of the guys in the group, or whoever was going to be the go-between, but at least she had started.

Now to get to work building it.

She could always buy the basic design, but if she wanted his site to be completely unique—and she did—she'd be better off doing it on her own.

Whether or not he was going to like the ideas she'd proposed, she didn't know, but that wouldn't change what she had to get done first. All the coding was going to be a pain in the ass and—

His reply was already in her inbox.

Come to the studio.

Arching a brow, she emailed him back. *Why?*

Barely a minute passed before she had his answer. *I want to see you.* In parentheses, it read, *And after that, I want to strip you naked and fuck you.*

Okay...that made something warm and delicious settle in her belly. But still. She needed to get a little bit of work done on this. And she knew she wouldn't get anything done if she didn't do it before she went in there to see Marc. *I'm working right now. I need to spend some time on this website design and I have to take care of a few others things too.*

Marc scowled at the message that came up on his iPhone.

He started to tap back a response and then stopped. "Screw this."

Standing, he headed out of the studio, prowling through the house until he found her.

He wasn't surprised when he saw her tucked away in the library. The room faced out over the water, but she had the blinds down and the curtains drawn. Her long, lean legs were tucked up with the laptop on her knees. She was sitting in one of the armchairs, keeping the mouse on the nearby table, and the look on her face told him she wasn't even aware of him. Brows down low over her eyes, a frown twisting her lips.

Leaning against the door, he crossed his arms over his chest and watched her.

Her hair, that dark brown hair with its threads of gold and red, kept falling into her eyes. That was when she noticed him, after she shoved her hair back and it fell right into her eyes two seconds later. She went to reach into her bag and she glanced up, a scarf in one hand.

Their gazes locked and Marc found himself thinking about how he'd woken up. Alone. She'd left a note on the bedside table. *Went running. Back in a while.*

So he'd gone into his studio, hoping she'd find him when she got back. Chaili had done long-distance running for years and it wasn't unusual for her to spend hours on a run, but he hadn't thought she'd go running and then hide herself away and work.

As she wrapped the scarf around her head, using it to tie her hair back, he shoved off the wall. "How come you're hiding away in here?" he asked.

"I'm not hiding away." She flipped the top of the computer around, showing him the screen. She tapped on it. "I'm working."

Marc stared at something that looked like a foreign language. One involving a lot of weird symbols and abbreviations. There were words in English and he was pretty certain it was supposed to make sense...but it didn't. He cocked his head to the left, then to the right, but that didn't help any. "If the job is trying to make sense out of that, you've got a lot of work left to do," he said. "It's Sunday... You do still take time off, right?"

With a slight grin, she flipped the screen back around. "That's code. For the website I'm building for you. You remember, the job you hired me to do? And I take time off when projects allow. Since I'm tight on time here, I'm going to have to take time off when I can manage it. I need to put in a few hours today, plus I still have to finish that rush job. I already committed to it."

He dropped onto the ottoman in front of her and reached out, laid a hand on one ankle.

She shivered, lashes drooping low over her eyes.

"You've already been working for a while, it looks like. How long ago did you get back from your run? You've already showered and everything."

"Ummm." Her gaze darted down. "Yeah...been back for a while. You were still sleeping so I showered in a different bathroom. Didn't want to wake you. Been working about an hour or so. I need to do a few more hours here or I'm not going to keep to the schedule I've set for myself."

"How much can you get done?" He tightened his grip on her ankle. "I mean, we need to talk to the guys, right? Do the photos and shit."

A soft breath hissed out of her as he dipped down and pressed his lips to her knee. "I can do plenty on the basic stuff. The...ah...coding."

Her fingers pushed into his hair, tightened. "Marc...?"

Tracing his tongue along her skin, he murmured, "Hmmm?"

"Are you serious about me doing your website or did you just decide to throw some work my way?"

Tensing, he sat up.

Her eyes glinted.

"What?"

"You heard me. Do you want this site done or not?"

"I need a new site, damn it. You've seen how shitty it looks, right?"

"Oh, yes. I've seen. But if you're serious, then you need to let me work when I say I'm working." She glanced down to where he was holding on to her ankle. "Would you be totally cool with it if I walked into the recording studio when you and the guys were working on a new album and just starting stripping out of my clothes?"

Slowly, he uncurled his fingers from her ankle. "I'm just..."

"Marc, I know what you're *just*...doing." Chaili kept her gaze focused on the computer. "And if I didn't need to have this done for you in a seriously short period of time, then we could *just* for as long as you want."

"If it's going to be too hard to get the website done by the deadline, we can put it off a few days," he said, blowing out a breath. Shoving upright, he started to pace.

"No. I said I could get it done. And the bonus happens only if I get it done by that time, remember?" She looked up long enough to flash him a quick smile. "I plan on getting it done."

"Yeah. I see that." Hooking a hand over the back of his neck, he glanced over at the clock. "How long are you going to work?"

"I'll need a break in a couple of hours. If I get enough done, I may stop for the day," she said.

"Okay. So...lunch?"

She smiled at him. "It's a date."

Chapter Fourteen

"I want to take you out tonight."

With the phone propped on her ear, Chaili continued to work on the pictures. So far, she'd finished up the pictures for Miguel, Seth and Mac. Jacob and Marc were all that was left. Jacob had been out of town and she'd get his done once he was back. She was nervous about working on Marc's, but that wasn't anything she could explain to him.

"Okay. Take me out where?" she asked.

"Blue's."

Chaili almost dropped the phone.

"Ah..." She licked her lips. She wasn't so certain she wanted to do that.

"Yes?"

"I don't have anything to wear." That wasn't a lie. Blue ran a classy joint and appearances were important. Chaili wasn't about to go in there without the right kind of armor. Clothing was armor in certain areas of life. Walking into the place where her ex had tried to humiliate her a couple of times...yeah. Armor was necessary.

"Maybe you could let me buy you something."

Chaili turned away from the computer after taking a few seconds to save her work. She rose from the computer and paced the floor of her living room, staring at nothing, seeing Marc's face in her mind.

For the past two weeks, they'd seen each other almost

every day and it felt like she was getting so deep in over her head...but she wasn't scared, because he seemed to be right there with her.

This, though...this was a hard thing he was asking.

"I'm not a member there anymore," she said quietly. "I can't afford the dues and I don't really want to be a member anymore."

"I am. You know how the place works, right? I'm at the select level. I can take guests, and I want you to be my guest." He paused and then added, "My date, Chaili. I'm taking you as my date...my woman, not my slave, not my submissive. I want to take you out to dinner, for drinks. I want to dance with you someplace where I don't have to worry about cameras or anything."

Swallowing, she moved over to the couch, thinking that through. "Is that all we're doing? Dinner. Drinks. Dancing?"

"I already told you I've got lines I won't cross...certain areas at Blue's, I haven't gone, and I won't go there." He blew out a breath and then added, "But if you want, I can see if she's got one of your rooms open."

"My..." It clicked and then she sighed. "No. I don't need that, Marc." Hell, it didn't seem necessary. Marc took her places with just his voice, just his hands. That extra kick in the kink factor wasn't needed anymore. "So this is basically just a date. Dinner. Drinks. Dancing. But you want the privacy thing, right?"

"Pretty much."

Nibbling on her lip, she thought it through. "Okay. But you're not buying me anything to wear. I'll go shopping." And she could actually do that too. Ilona had sent her an advance and she only felt a little bit guilty keeping some of the money. It was a hell of a lot of money, more than she'd expected to see in the next six months. Wasn't wrong to spend a little bit of it on clothes.

"I want to buy you something."

"No." She didn't feel right with it. Hedging away from the insistent command she heard in his voice, she offered the most practical reason imaginable. "I'm not that easy to find clothes for these days. The mastectomy made certain of that."

"That didn't go well," he muttered.

He hadn't wanted her spending her money on clothes for a date, Marc thought.

Standing in the middle of the store, looking around, he eyed the mannequins and tried to picture one of the dresses on Chaili. Shit. He'd planned on just getting her sizes, but...

Okay.

That plan was out. But he was buying her something.

A long, slender woman clad all in black approached him. She had a polite, professional mask in place and looked almost as lifeless as one of the mannequins. But he figured she'd be a good person to ask.

"Is there anything I can help you with?"

Once he'd made his purchase, he shouldered through the doors and started down Michigan Avenue. He needed to put in a call to Blue. She had private dining booths and he wanted one. He wanted to make sure nothing would go wrong tonight.

A real date.

He hadn't taken Chaili on a real date yet.

Well, they'd managed to grab a very late movie the other day. That had been fun.

The movie had sucked and they'd ended up making out for most of it. Which had been the best part, if you asked him.

Maybe they could try—

"Hello, Marc."

The sound of that voice managed to poke a needle in the nice, happy little bubble he'd wrapped around himself. Stopping in the middle of the sidewalk, he found himself looking at a face he barely recognized.

Three years ago, Lily had been on the border of too skinny. Beautiful, but almost painfully skinny. White-blonde hair that was almost always impeccably coifed, big blue eyes with perfect makeup, set against porcelain skin. She'd looked like a doll, he realized. Yeah, she'd been beautiful, but like a doll. A very breakable one. He just hadn't realized it.

Now, with her hair cut in a short, sleek style, it's color a warmer gold, her face free of makeup and her curves almost generous, she looked...well. Rather lovely. More beautiful, he decided. And steady. Steadier than he'd ever seen her.

"Hello, Lily."

She glanced around and then nodded to the coffee shop to the right. "Do you have a minute? I saw you coming out of Neiman Marcus and wanted to speak with you."

Sighing, he glanced around. "Lily..."

"Please. It won't take long."

"You look well," he said. They sat tucked in the back of the coffee shop, his back to the crowd. Lily drank some sort of frothy concoction that had more sugar than caffeine. He drank coffee, black, and wished he'd thought to get an extra shot of espresso.

"Hmm. Well, sometimes I'm still not so crazy about who I see in the mirror, but I'm trying. Thanks for giving me a few minutes. I really need to do this, you know."

"Do what?" he asked warily. He couldn't help it. This woman had come so close to fucking up his life. So close.

"Apologize." She stared at him levelly. "I...well, you know I'd been using. I was good at hiding it. But after that night..." She shrugged. "You can't hide it very well after you're in the hospital for an overdose, right?"

"Are you clean now?"

"Yes." She gave him a small smile...a proud one. "Two years now. There were some slips and slides that first year, but two years clean. It's the longest I've ever gone and I'm going to make it stick this time."

"Good."

She nodded. "Well, then. About that apology..."

"You've already apologized," he said tersely.

"It's not the same," she said, shaking her head. "Over the phone. In a letter. I went there with the intent to try and ruin you if you wouldn't do what I wanted, even though I was the one who screwed up. With everything..." She stopped, looking away. "I screwed up with everything. But you were one of my worst mistakes. I was so wrong to do that to you and I'm sorry."

Marc stared down at his coffee. How the hell did he respond to this? *It's okay?* Well, that wasn't exactly right. *Don't worry about it...?* That didn't seem right, either. Blowing out a breath, he thought through the possible answers, turning each of them over. An apology was offered...usually somebody offered it because they wanted forgiveness. And yeah, he could do that.

Okay, then.

"I forgive you," he said, still staring at his coffee. He shot another look at her and then focused back on his coffee. "That doesn't mean I'm looking to reestablish any sort of relationship here, Lily. I think you and I were bad for each other. But I forgive you."

"Thank you." Her words were a soft, watery whisper.

A moment later, her chair scraped back against the floor. She paused by his side, her hand resting on his arm. He held rigid as she dipped her head, pressed her lips to his temple. When she left a few seconds later, he blew out a breath. Then, lifting his coffee to his lips, he pondered the chair where she'd been sitting.

Well, that was one little chapter of his life he figured he could consider closed.

Not that it had much mattered to him. He was ready to focus all of his attention on Chaili, this woman who had suddenly become his everything.

The black dress had been a miracle of a find. It was halter-style, but with a loose, draping effect that looked pretty decent. The skirt hit a few inches above the knee and when she spun around, it flared out nicely. She debated on wearing any stockings and decided, *what the hell*. Marc had liked them. She didn't bother with the garter belt, though. Black panties. Nude stockings with the lacy, stay-up tops. A pair of her good black heels that she hadn't been able to part with it... The soles were screaming hot pink and just sliding them on made her smile.

She was standing in front of the mirror, finishing up her makeup, when he knocked.

After one last glance, she headed toward the door, smiling at the way her heels clicked on the floor. A date. Her belly fluttered a little. She was going on a date with Marc. To Blue's. Yeah, it was just dinner and dancing, but still.

The very atmosphere of Blue's was like a hedonistic delight, one she'd never been able to enjoy the way she would have liked, thanks to...

"No," she whispered as she stopped in front of the door. "Not anymore."

All she had to do was refuse to open the door. She wasn't opening the door...in her head.

Marc knocked again. She was damn well opening the door for him. And with a smile, she did so.

Her heart jumped up into her throat when she saw him.

He'd gotten his hair cut. Trimmed it so that the long lengths weren't tumbling into his face. And he'd shaved. Nothing hid that beautiful face, not a damn thing.

Golden eyes gleamed at her as he looked her over from head to toe. "You look amazing."

"Ah...you do, too," she said, licking her lips.

A wicked grin slanted his lips. "What do you have on under the dress?"

She winked at him and then tugged up the hem, revealing the lacy top of one stocking.

"Hmmm." He reached over, laid a hand on her thigh, stroking up. "Nice."

She held her breath, waiting.

But then he backed away. "Are you ready?"

Well, damn.

"Yeah. I just need to grab my purse." Pout for a minute.

He waited on the porch while she did it and when she turned to lock the door, he crowded her up against it, dragging her skirt up, nudging his cock against the silken strip of her panties. "I'd like to come in," he whispered against her neck. "But if I do that, I won't take you out. And I want to take you out."

A shiver raced through her as he pumped against her, raking his teeth along her neck.

"Ah...you can always come in later."

"True."

A few seconds later, he let go. She remained against the door, her brow pressed to the glass as she waited for her breathing to calm. "You're mean, sometimes, you know that, Marc?"

"Yeah. This isn't news, though," he said.

She turned around, smoothing her skirt down, and eyed him narrowly. He had an unrepentant look on his face and his eyes all but burned with hunger as he stared at her. As she moved past him, she brushed the back of her hand against the ridge of his cock, smiling a little as his breath hissed out of him.

Her smile widened when she saw what he'd driven.

She didn't know enough about cars to know what it was, but it wasn't the sleek, sexy little sports car. Nor was it one of his bikes. No, this was his SUV. Nice. Roomy. With tinted windows. As he opened the door for her, she turned and gave him a guileless smile. "Do we need to be there at a particular time?"

Marc pushed his hand into her hair, stroking down to her neck absently and massaging. "Yeah. But not until dinner. That's at eight."

"Maybe want to drive up by the lake?"

He lifted a brow and then shrugged.

Smiling at him, she slid into the SUV, clicked her seatbelt.

Once he'd pulled out of the neighborhood where she lived with Shera, Chaili reached over, laid a hand on his thigh. Stroked upward. He hissed out a breath. As she started to stroke him, she closed her eyes.

Marc groaned as she dragged his zipper down.

Parked on the side of the road, his hands gripping her head, he rasped, "If a cop sees us, we'll be lucky if this doesn't end up on the news."

"Then you need to watch for cops," she whispered, opening her lips and taking him into the hot, wet cave of her mouth.

Watch for cops, he thought, half dazed as she licked. Stroked. Sucked. Staring out the window, when he could be looking at her?

A car whizzed by and he jerked his head up, following it with his eyes for a moment and then lowering his gaze to stare at her. She hummed as she sucked on him. Licked. Nibbled at the flared head.

Over and over, working his length deeper, deeper...

He tangled his hand in her hair when she stopped and groaned, arching his hips upward and growling, "Don't stop there, baby. Take more."

She lifted her head a little and then slid back down. Slow. Excruciating.

But always stopping just a little short...

"Damn it, Chaili," he growled.

She lifted her head, kneeling on the seat, nose to nose with him. Her mouth was red, plump. "This is my game," she whispered. "I'm playing this time."

Groaning, he slammed his head back against the padded headrest of the seat, certain he was going to die of a heart attack if she kept this up. "Play it then, before I decided to take the lead."

"No, it's my game," she whispered again, as she went back down. Taking him in her mouth again. That amazing, wonderful mouth...

A little faster this time and she wrapped her fingers around the base, stroking. Teasing. Slamming against the door, he stared blindly out the window, arching to meet each movement as his hand cradled the back of her head.

So damned good, so...yeah... "Damn it, Chaili, if you stop, I'm going to paddle you, you hear me?" he snarled as he felt the movements of her head slow.

She made another one of those little humming sounds in her throat. And kept moving. Faster. Taking him deeper. "Yeah, just like..."

Another car sped by. Marc groaned. Shuddered.

She lifted up, slightly, nipped the head of his cock and then fell back into her rhythm. Taking him deeper, harder, until she was all but swallowing him with each stroke. Then, as another car went speeding by, she tugged on his balls, hard.

With a hoarse shout, he came.

Chaili sat next to him with a cat's smile on her face, looking about as pleased he'd ever seen her.

He reached over, covered the hand she had on her thigh. "I'm crazy about you."

Her gaze swung his way, a startled look in her eyes. Then she grinned, shrugged. "Well. I'll be sure to give you impromptu blowjobs more often."

"Well..." He squinted at her and then looked back at the road. "I'm not going to argue with that, but that's got nothing to do with it." He thought about the picture he still carried in his pocket. About the stuff he'd taken from his sister's house. He should let her know he had it.

Just...not yet. He was still adjusting to everything he was feeling about her. Still trying to wrap his head around it, and it was powerful stuff. Very powerful.

Everything else paled in comparison. Everybody else...

Frowning, he thought about earlier. Lily. Shit. Was that something he should mention?

Well. Duh. Yes. The answer seemed pretty clear, because he knew if she'd run into that asshole ex of hers, he'd want to know. Yeah, they weren't exactly at the stage where they were talking about a future...

A future.

His brain fuzzed out on him and he realized he was thinking about thoughts he'd never let himself contemplate before.

A future. With Chaili.

Oh. Damn. He was in trouble. Completely the right kind of trouble, for once. But no way, no how was he prepared for this.

Something they maybe needed to figure out.

A talk for tomorrow. They'd talk about that, he'd let her know about Lily. Because there was no way he was going to mention Lily right after she'd just given him the best blowjob of his life.

From the outside, Blue's place looked like a posh sort of club. Maybe a restaurant or something.

But one had to flash a membership ID to get through the doors, and those memberships weren't cheap. Chaili could remember how much Tim had chucked out for the basic. The basic level got you inside the doors. Tim had made decent money—he was a junior partner at his dad's law firm, thus the need for discretion. But he still hadn't been able to afford anything more than the basic membership and the occasional jaunt to the other floors.

Marc had a higher level. Obviously.

He pulled up at an entrance she hadn't seen and before she could even open the door, somebody else was there doing it for her, a man dressed in black who gave her what looked like a polite little bow.

"Hey, Hank."

"Mr. Archer, a pleasure to see you." The man gave Marc a smile that looked pretty damn genuine as he accepted Marc's keys.

Chaili glanced at the door in front of them, eyeing it curiously.

As they headed toward it, two more men appeared, coming out of the shadows, quietly, again giving both Marc and Chaili that polite little nod. As the doors opened, she saw a set of stairs, an elevator and a hallway. She could hear the beat and throb of music and she smiled a little. Dancing...with Marc.

"You want to dance before we go upstairs?"

She glanced to the elevator. "Ah...upstairs?"

"VIP levels are on the top floor," he murmured in her ear. "We'll be dining there."

Ahhh, she hadn't known that. "Sure. Let's go dance."

There was no way in the world she was going to miss out on a chance to dance with Marc.

While it might look like a posh sort of club or restaurant on the outside, once you got inside, especially once you hit the dance floor, anybody with eyes would see the difference.

Chaili wasn't too concerned with their surroundings, though. She'd been to Blue's often enough that it no longer surprised her. On the dance floor, just about anything *could* happen...except sex. As long as the partner was willing.

There were stages elevated if somebody wanted to put on a show, and all of them were occupied. Several floggings were being done. One woman was being bound, a very complicated form of bondage—she thought it was kinbaku, but she wasn't sure. It was a lot more than just tying her hands behind her back, though.

There were a few submissives being disciplined on the floor.

Mostly, people were dancing.

Marc pulled her into his arms and she went, sliding her arms around his neck, glad she'd worn the heels. She was eye to eye with him now. Staring into those golden eyes that had haunted her dreams for so many years.

He flicked his gaze past her, his eyes lingering on the stage. She followed his glance, saw that he was watching the woman being bound. "I think I'd like to do that to you," he murmured.

Chaili smiled and leaned in, pressed her lips to his ear. "I think I'd like to have you do it."

He turned his face in to her hair and breathed her in. "You know, I'm trying to figure out how I didn't find you before now."

Chaili closed her eyes and tucked her head against his chest. She'd been right here. Wishing for him. Waiting. Dreaming. But he'd never seen her.

No point in regretting it, though. Especially when she had all she ever wanted right here.

One song bled into another. Some faster, some slower. But Marc never let her leave the circle of his arms, and she was just fine with that. As the music once more fell into a slow rhythm, slow and sensual, he tugged her even closer, pushing his thigh between hers, dragging the material of her skirt up so that nothing separated her from him but the material of her panties and his trousers.

The beat of the music sank into her, almost as powerful as the music Marc could make. He moved her in time to it, the hard muscles of his thigh rubbing over her until she was shuddering, just from that.

"You're getting wet," he whispered, one hand splayed low over her spine. "I feel it."

She turned her head to say something...anything.

But his mouth came crushing down on hers. As she opened for him, his tongue pushed inside. Demanding. In. Out. Stabbing into the depths of her mouth, a rhythm that was unmistakable. She was panting by the time he lifted his head. "I'll be doing that to you soon. Very soon."

Unable to resist teasing him, she whispered, "And what if there aren't any rooms?"

You had to have a room if you wanted to engage in sex at Blue's. It was the one hard and fast rule and she stuck to it. People could get banned for it, their memberships permanently revoked.

Those golden eyes just glittered at her.

"Not an issue," he promised.

The need almost made her knees buckle.

"You ready to go upstairs?" he whispered, his breath ghosting over her skin.

She couldn't find the breath to speak. So she just nodded.

If they'd gotten to the steps five seconds sooner, they would have missed him. If they'd bothered working through the crowd to the velvet rope that separated the VIP's entrance, they would have missed him. But the main area was closer and as they mounted the steps to the third floor, he was heading down.

The music from the dance floor was muted at this level, although she wished it were blasting. Deafening her.

Tim stared at her for a long moment. Then he cut his eyes toward Marc, his mouth twisting in a sneer before he jerked his gaze back to her. "Back to your usual, it looks like," Tim said.

"Not hardly," she said. "After all, I moved past you."

Marc moved a little closer, his hand resting at the base of her spine. "Come on. We're not here to mess with fools like him."

"Why are you here? Ready to get your freak back on?" Tim jeered. "Yeah, I know you had to let your membership lapse and all. Probably raring to go after all this time. And you got one hell of a money train going now, don't you?"

Marc let go of her. Moved around her. She caught his arm. "Stop it," she said quietly. "He's not worth it and we both know it."

Marc shrugged her away.

"You have a very, very short memory," Marc said quietly. Snaking out a hand, he jerked Tim forward, glaring into the shorter man's face. "Do I need to get you a refresher on what I was going to do to you if you mentioned her name again?"

"You can't," Tim sneered. "You know the rules here."

"Well, the thing about being a money train, you can buy your way out of a lot of trouble," Marc whispered softly.

"Damn it, Marc," Chaili said. "Enough."

He turned his head, looked at her.

Her blue eyes, blazing like flames against the soft gold of her skin, snapped at him. "He's not worth it."

"You are," he said softly.

She closed her eyes, caught her breath. A few seconds later, she opened them and then looked at him. "Then let him go. If I'm worth this, then I'm worth letting him go. He doesn't mean anything to me, and neither do his words."

"Don't they?" he asked, searching her face. He kept thinking of the sadness he saw. The lingering pain.

"No." She moved closer, resting a hand on his arm. "You mean a hell of a lot more than he ever could...ever did. Don't you know that by now?"

Heavy footsteps sounded on the steps above them. Blowing out his breath, Marc uncurled his grip from the man's shirt, shoving him away. "You get this walk," he warned him. "But don't keep pushing your luck."

He didn't bother to watch as Tim disappeared, just focused on Chaili's eyes, those amazing eyes. "I won't keep letting him mouth off like that. He'll go too far."

"Yeah. Probably. But not here." She leaned in, pressed her lips to his. "Come on, didn't we have a date on the top floor?"

It was 7:38 when they got to the room.

It was 7:39 when Marc had her pressed back against the door.

It was 7:40 when he had her cuffed, the cuffs hooked over a convenient little hook fastened into the door.

It was 7:41 when he had her knees hooked over his elbows as he pushed inside her. "I told you I'd be doing this soon," he said, his voice a low, throaty purr in the stunning silence of the room.

It was one of the private rooms, Chaili had noticed that, but unlike any of the rooms she'd seen before.

Dazed, stunned, she stared into his eyes as he continued to burrow deeper inside her. Next to no warning. Just in the room, and...bam. Arms stretched over her head, her legs hooked over his forearms as he fucked her...she sucked in a desperate breath and whimpered his name.

"Say it like that again," he said, his voice calm, easy. Like he was ordering a pizza or something. "I like it when you say my name all broken like that."

Groaning, she bucked in his arms and tried to ride the ridge of his cock. But he held back, watching her. Waiting.

"I want to hear you whimpering," he whispered. He started to shaft her with slow, teasing little strokes that did nothing to assuage the fire inside her. "You're so fucking beautiful, Chaili. Let me hear it. Give it to me..."

She cried out, squeezing her eyes closed as his name fell from her lips.

"That's it..." He slid deeper. Withdrew. Pushed in. Harder this time, so that the flared head of his cock rasped over the sensitive bundle of nerves buried in her pussy. "Come on...do it again. I want to see you break for me."

She jerked against the cuffs, clamped down around him and tried to keep him inside her.

He surged deeper. Harder. "Break for me, baby girl," he growled. "Break..."

Chaili shuddered, feeling it rise inside, taking her deeper, deeper. Harder. Harder. As he moved...harder, harder...deeper, deeper.

Her heart couldn't take it. Couldn't handle it. Couldn't

handle it. Like it was going to explode, shatter...and she thought maybe *she* was...oh, oh!

He growled, slamming inside her. "Come for me," he rasped, his mouth crushing into hers, tongue thrusting past her lips to take her mouth the same way he took her body.

She shuddered. Quaked.

And as he drove into her once more, she climaxed.

Chaili stared at the silvery strands in the box.

"Marc...I...I can't..."

He pulled them out of the box. "Why?" He held one of them up to her ears, smiling a little. "They'll look good on you."

"I...just. Well."

"We've been going out for over two weeks. I think that means I'm allowed to buy you a present."

"Is that in the dating handbook?"

He tugged on her hair. "Well, for it to be official, I think I have to ask you to go steady..." He leaned and brushed her hair back. "So, tell me something, Chaili, you wanna go steady with me?" he teased.

He might have been teasing, but it still managed to settle a lump in her throat. Swallowing around it, she looked down, staring at the box so she wouldn't give herself away. "I think we're a little past the high school drama stuff, aren't we?"

Marc shrugged. "Hell, out of high school, maybe. But the drama stuff, does that ever end? And I'm not entirely joking..." He laid a hand on her cheek. "There's something real here. You know it. I feel it. We don't need to put a name to it, but I'm not planning on walking away from this."

Something real.

Hell. She didn't need to put a name to it, because she already knew what it was.

Shaken, she focused on the earrings again. Easier that way. "I'm just not really comfortable accepting gifts, Marc," she said quietly.

"It's just one," he pointed out.

Rising from the couch, she tucked the earrings inside the box. Something told her she needed to be careful here. Maybe not do anything. Yet. This was a scary conversation to have.

"Just one gift," she blurted out. "Yeah. But..." Her mind spun around, desperate to seize onto something.

Something real...something real. She wanted to believe that so bad. Wanted to believe they'd still be spending so much time together after the website was done. But what about when he went back to the studio? Back on tour...

The website—

"The website!" She turned around and glared at him.

A wary look entered his eyes. "What about the website?"

"You all but handed me the easiest job in the world and you're overpaying me!" Okay, that was stretching it. It wasn't easy and she was damn well busting her ass. Maybe he was overpaying her...

"Hey, we've already agreed the damn website I've got is a joke," he said, his voice edgy. "I needed the damn thing redone, right?"

"Well, you didn't need to pay me double what it's worth," she babbled. *Okay, I'm being silly here...*

"How in the hell do I know what they're worth?" he asked. "I named a figure and we agreed on it and it's not like it's a handout if you're doing the damned work!"

A handout—

Fury flickered, flared to life inside her. Okay. She'd been reaching when she threw the website out there, but... "A handout?" she said quietly.

Marc's face went rigid.

"That implies like you think I might need a handout," she said coldly. She was broke, yeah, but damn it, *he* didn't need to know that.

"I'm not giving you a damned handout. I needed a damn job done and I asked the one person I knew who could do it to get it done," he said.

"Huh. And oddly enough, you managed to toss out a figure that all but wiped out a few of my medical bills." Narrowing her eyes, she asked, "When did you see my medical bills, Marc?"

He didn't say anything.

"You son of a bitch."

Chapter Fifteen

Things could go from heaven to hell in the blink of an eye and Marc had no idea just how this had happened.

He'd just wanted to give her something.

That was all.

But as she stormed around the private room at Blue's, gathering up the clothes he'd stripped off her, he realized he'd managed to piss her off but good.

And he didn't know how.

She was leaving. *Why?*

She's running, a small voice in the back of his head whispered not even a second later.

Running?

He remembered the panicked fear he'd glimpsed in her eyes just moments ago, before it had faded. Faded? Or had she hidden it? He'd thought they were done hiding things, but was she still...

Okay. She was either hiding still, or he'd fucked things up.

Either way, he wasn't letting her walk away like this.

As she pulled her dress on, he snagged his trousers and tugged them up. Checked his pocket. Yep. It was there.

She started for the door, but he beat her, just barely. As she tried to jerk it open, he slammed it shut over her head. "Running away?" he asked softly.

"No. I'm leaving. I can't believe you fucking did that, Marc," she snarled.

"What? Have you take over a job you should have been doing all along?" He shrugged. "Shoot me. The way I see it, the bonus doesn't even cover the money you would have made if you had been doing the site all this time, like you *should* have been doing. It's fair enough, in my mind."

She whirled around and glared at him. "Why didn't you just *ask* me?"

"Ask you what?" he said bluntly. "Ask you to take the job? I *did* that, remember?"

She narrowed her eyes at him.

"Oh, wait, now let me guess. You'd rather I point it out like this... *Chaili, I know you're tight on money. And I really do need you back on my website. Can you come back?* Shit, you'd never think one had nothing to do with the other."

"Are you're telling me they didn't?"

"I never knew you weren't doing it!" he shouted. "And if you had been doing it, the way you should have been, you wouldn't be so fucking tight on money! And if I didn't have my head up my ass, I would have realized what was going on! And it still doesn't change the fact that you did the best job on the damned site and I needed you back."

"So. You just overpaid me on accident."

He glared at her. "You're running away because you're scared."

"I am not," she snapped. "I'm leaving because I can't stand a man who thinks he can control me like that."

"If I'd wanted to control you, I would have just paid off every last one of the fucking medical bills," he said. "And it damn well killed me not to do it. It's making me sick thinking about how hard you've had it, damn it. But I didn't do that. I

220

gave you a job that I needed you to do."

She just curled her lip at him. "I don't need the pity work, Marc. Or the pity fuck. So if you'd just move..." She turned back to the door expectantly.

Reaching into his pocket, he pulled out the picture. Slammed it against the door. "No," he rasped. Pressing his lips to the back of her head, he whispered again, "You're not doing this, Chaili. I'm not letting you run away over whatever in the hell has just scared you. I just found you, damn it."

Chaili jumped as his hand slammed against the door. One arm came around her, hauled her back against him. She jerked against his hold, but he continued to hold her. "You've got my head all screwed up. You've got me twisted up in knots and there are things I want to say to you, but I know I'm going to fuck up what I'm saying."

As he scooped her up in his arms, she went rigid. *I'm not doing this. I'm not. Damn it. How could he have gone through my stuff, found out about the bills...* Her belly was hot and tight with shame, just thinking about it.

"I didn't mean to see the bills," he said as he sat on the couch. "I was working on a song, the day we were at your place, with the scarves. I accidentally knocked the bills over. That's how I saw them."

Staring at anything but him, Chaili told herself it didn't matter. He'd seen private stuff. He shouldn't have looked—

Shit, what was he supposed to do? Leave it on the floor? I could have put it away...

Shit. She was being a coward. Closing her eyes, she said quietly, "Let me go, Marc. I need to think."

"You mean run away," he muttered.

"No. I mean think."

As his arms fell away, she scooted off his lap, but she didn't get up, just curled up on the couch, her head pressed against her knees. Okay. He'd seen the medical bills. Nothing she could do about that. And she was being stupid here. Stupid, and she knew it. She...

Hell, she was terrified.

She wanted to believe he felt something *real*, because that meant it could be something that lasted but...

"Marc," she said, glancing up at him. But he wasn't looking at her.

He was looking at something he held in his hand.

Slowly, he held it up, flipped it around so she could see it. Startled, she hissed out a breath, shooting a look between him and the picture. It was one of the ones she'd stripped out of her house. One of the dozens. This one, one of her...and him. Down at the pier. He'd been laughing, playfully leering at her and she'd been pushing him away. She'd given the pictures to Shera, though. "Ah...did Shera give you that?"

"No." He stroked the edge of the picture with his finger. "I found it...with a box of everything else that was us. Or me. You decided to cut me out of your life. Right after I realized just how important you were to mine."

Right after I realized...

Licking her lips, she whispered, "When did you find it?"

"The day I came looking for you at that idiot's party."

Tears blurred her eyes. She blinked them away. That had been more than two weeks ago. Her heart skipped a beat. Okay. This conversation was taking a turn she wasn't prepared for. She needed a drink. Yeah. Some coffee. Something to clear her brain. She was slightly tipsy from the wine they'd had at dinner.

Drunk on sex. Emotions kiting way too high. "I need some coffee," she said, shoving to her feet and heading for the small kitchenette the private VIP rooms boasted.

Two arms came around her, hauling her back against that lean, muscled body. Marc's silken black hair brushed up against her cheek. "What are you doing, Chaili?" he whispered. "Why do you keep running?"

"I'm not. I just need some coffee." Her voice came out a bare whisper. *I need to think...need to...* Oh, hell. He pressed his hand against her belly, his thumb stroking up, down.

"Every time I try to tell what I've got trapped inside me, you either run away or try to hide or change the subject. Now..." He dipped his head, nuzzled the curve between her neck and shoulder. "Now you want to make coffee. Chaili, have I ever mentioned that you confuse the hell out of me sometimes?"

Coffee, she told herself. *Caffeine.* She needed to think.

"Why are you still *trying* to run?" he whispered.

Because I need to think! "I..."

She licked her lips. Lifting her hands, she covered his, staring down at the way her hands looked on his. And she saw her ring. That ring that Shera had made for her. *You think things through too hard.* And here she was, doing it again.

Groaning, she dropped her head back on his shoulder. "Maybe I confuse you, but you terrify me."

For the longest time, he didn't say anything.

Then, finally, he turned her around, his hands curved around her waist, his gaze intent on hers. Slowly, he slid one hand up, up, up...lingering over the scars hidden under her dress, tracing the tattoo he couldn't see. Along her neck until he cupped her face. "Why?"

"Because." She licked her lips, staring into his face, even

223

though she *really* wanted to run and hide now. "Damn it, Marc. You're everything I've ever wanted. You're what I've *always* wanted. And now you're standing there like maybe I could really have you and it scares me. What if I lost you?"

He cupped her face.

Her heart slammed against her ribs. Okay. He wasn't pulling away. Wasn't looking at her like he was about to wig out. That...that was a good thing, she thought.

"I spent years searching for what I wanted...and I just found her. The fucked up thing is that you were here all along. There hasn't been anybody who has made me feel the way you do, Chaili," he said quietly. "Nobody. You let me feel like I can be me. You make me feel real. Over the past few years, I've forgotten what it's like to feel real."

Well, that wasn't a shiny declaration of love, but it sounded pretty promising.

She reached up and curled her hands into his shirt. "You are real, Marc. You're a real boy, I promise you."

"Smart ass," he whispered. His other hand came up, until he had her face cupped in his palms. "I don't feel like myself half the time. I don't feel...like me. But with you, it's different. You make me feel like it's okay to be who I am. What I am."

Her throat ached as she tugged him closer. Easing up onto her toes, she pressed a kiss to the stubbled line of his jaw. "Marc, baby...there's nothing wrong with who you are. What you are. I adore the man you are. Well, except when you're being sneaky and trying to find ways to take care of me."

"I can't help that," he said sourly. "I want to take care of you. I kind of need it." He fisted a hand in her hair, tugged her head back. "And there's this way you look at me that makes me...even better than I know I am. Makes me want to *be* better.

"Chaili..." His gaze roamed over her face. He squeezed his

eyes closed, dipped his head until his brow rested against her. "I'm going to screw this up."

Burrowing in close, she rested her head on his shoulder. "Well, if it helps, I've already screwed up a little. I'm sorry I jumped on you. I...um. I panicked. I'm sorry. I just keep thinking something's going to fall apart and I just want to run away before that happens. I'm terrified something will fall apart and that you're never going to feel the way I do and..."

Chaili gasped out as he backed her up. The wall was at her back, and the long, powerful lines of his body pressed against her front, the heat of him burning through her dress. Fire seemed to burn in the depths of his eyes.

"I love you," he snarled. "Stop worrying, and stop running. I love you, damn it. I don't know how or when it happened, but I know it's real, and I know it's there. I love you, Chaili. Just you. Only you."

As she tried to catch her breath, as she tried to catch the heart that seemed to have fallen to her knees, Marc stood there, one arm braced on the wall by her head, his face twisted in a brooding, challenging scowl. *I love you...*

She'd heard that.

I love you...

Just you...

Only you...

The rest of it was still a jumble of words her brain struggled to make sense of, but *those* words, she understood.

"Damn it," he said, his voice a harsh, ragged demand. "Say something."

Chaili didn't know *what* to say. Licking her lips, she opened her mouth, but nothing wanted to come out. He'd said it...the words she'd held trapped inside her for so long, he'd just said them to her. Shaken, she reached up and cupped his face in her hands, stroking one thumb across the curve of his lower lip. The rasp of stubble scratched against her palm.

I love you…

"If you don't say something in the next five seconds, I'm going to go out of my mind," he said, his voice easy, almost level now. And his eyes were still burning as he stared down at her. "I just wanted you to know that."

A laugh bubbled out of her and she wrapped her arms around him. "Damn it, can you just give me a minute? I've only been waiting to hear you say that for half my life."

He shuddered, cuddling her close. Feeling that lean body against hers, feeling it tremble, she slid a hand under his shirt, stroked his back. "This is real, right?" she whispered. "You're serious?"

Marc pressed a kiss to the nape of her neck. "I'm not sure if I've ever been this serious about anything. Except…"

"Except what?" She lifted her head, staring at him.

Golden eyes bored into hers. A faint grin crooked his lips and he shrugged. "Well, if you keep trying to run away from me, I'm going to do something desperate. Like shackle you to me or something."

A half hysterical giggle escaped her. "Okay. No more running," she whispered, leaning in. She lifted her hands, cradling his face and pressing her lips to his. She wanted to remember each and every moment. Treasure each and every moment. Find a way to commit it all to memory. The feel of the stubble rasping against her palms. The intensity of his eyes, even the biting impatience she could see in his gaze. "No shackles needed, Marc. I've been waiting right here…for years. I've loved you for so long, I can't remember a time when I *didn't* love you."

Author's Note

Inspired by Marc Cohn's "Walking in Memphis" and The Scar Project...

www.thescarproject.org

About the Author

Shiloh Walker has been writing since she was a kid. She fell in love with vampires with the book Bunnicula and has worked her way up to the more...ah...serious works of fiction. She loves reading and writing just about every kind of romance. Once upon a time she worked as a nurse, but now she writes full time and lives with her family in the Midwest. She writes romantic suspense and paranormal romance, and urban fantasy under the name J.C. Daniels.

To learn more, please visit her Website (shilohwalker.com) or join her newsletter (shilohwalker.fanbridge.com).

Also, check her out on Facebook (AuthorShilohWalker) and Twitter (@shilohwalker)!

You can always come home. Second chances come a little harder.

A Forever Kind of Love
© *2011 Shiloh Walker*

Chase and Zoe were the high school golden couple. Football captain, cheerleader, prom royalty. After graduation, though, Chase couldn't resist the urge to experience life outside their small town. He didn't exactly expect Zoe to wait twelve years for him, but now that he's back, he finds some small part of him hoping she did.

It's no big surprise she's married. The kick in the face is she married his best friend.

Zoe was devastated when Chase left, but she's filed those bittersweet memories under "Moved On". She loves her life, and loves her husband. She has all she needs. And Chase keeps an honorable distance.

One cold, wet, miserable day, tragedy turns Zoe's world upside down. Chase never expected her to simply fall into his arms, but a man can dream. Except his dream doesn't include the fact that this time, she's the one hitting the road...and he's the one left behind.

Warning: This story contains heartbreak, heartache and one last chance for two lovers to find each other.

Available now in ebook from Samhain Publishing.

They've got the sex factor in spades.
But can love survive the "ex" factor?

Knowing the Ropes
© *2013 Teresa Noelle Roberts*

Selene has harbored kinky, submissive fantasies most of her life, but her experience as a domestic abuse counselor leaves her leery of giving up that much control. Case in point: the ex-fiancé she didn't love quite enough to test the limits of trust.

At a BDSM meet-and-greet, she sets out to learn how far is too far. Nick seems like the ideal dom to show her the ins and outs of ropes, floggers, and paddles—with no commitment clause.

After losing a sub he loved too much, Selene's country girl common sense and smoking sensuality is like a dream that Nick never dared to have—a perfect blend of kink and long-term domestic bliss.

Yet it's tough to figure out just how far they can push their limits when they've both agreed to a no-strings affair. Especially when an ex needs Nick's muscle and Selene's counseling skills to get out of a dangerous situation. By then it may be too late for love to survive all the things they're afraid to say.

Warning: Sexy, kinky, geeky dominant guy. Smart submissive woman. Crazy ex. A little experimentation between girlfriends. And lots and lots of kinky sex.

Available now in ebook and print from Samhain Publishing.

SAMHAIN
PUBLISHING

It's all about the story...

Romance

HORROR

Retro
ROMANCE

www.samhainpublishing.com

PB F WAL   11/14

Walker, Shiloh.

Beautiful scars /

F

CPSIA information can be obtained
at www.ICGtesting.com
Printed in the USA
FFOW01n1306230914
7480FF

9 781619 216334